Jessi and the Superbrat

**Look for these and other books
in the Baby-Sitters Club series:**

Jessi and the Superbrat
Ann M. Martin

AN
APPLE
PAPERBACK

SCHOLASTIC INC.
New York Toronto London Auckland Sydney

The author
would again like to thank
Jan Carr
for her help
in writing this book.

Cover art by Hodges Soileau

ISBN 0-590-42502-1

12 11 10 9 8 7 6   2 3 4/9

Printed in the U.S.A.   40

First Scholastic printing, September 1989

CHAPTER 1

"Mama! Daddy! Get in here! Jessi, hurry! Come on!"

That was my little sister, Becca, calling us from the living room. If you don't know Becca, you might've thought some major catastrophe had just happened, like:

A. The house was on fire.

B. Enemy soldiers had trooped into our yard, aimed their guns through the front window, and opened fire.

C. A flying saucer had crashed through our roof, and Martians were streaming down the staircase to capture us and take us off to Spacecreatureland.

So what was it? Fortunately, the answer was: None of the Above. The truth was, Becca was only calling us because of a TV show. The show had just come on and she wanted us to watch it with her.

Mama, Daddy, Squirt, and I were in the

kitchen, cleaning up after dinner. Well, Squirt wasn't exactly cleaning up. He was still strapped in his high chair, gnawing on a teething biscuit, and he had as much food caked on his face as we had just washed off the dishes.

Maybe I should introduce myself and my family before I start the story. My full name is Jessica Davis Ramsey, but everybody calls me Jessi. I'm eleven years old and in sixth grade. I'm black, and just to give you an idea of how few black families live here in Stoneybrook, Connecticut, I'll tell you that I'm the only black kid in my entire grade at Stoneybrook Middle School. I keep my hair long because I take ballet class two times a week and ballerinas are supposed to be able to pull their hair back. Probably my best feature is my legs. They're long, long, *long*, which is great for dancing. My grandma always says they're graceful, too. And Mama says I move like a cat. I take that as a compliment.

You can tell I have a nice family. I live with my parents, eight-year-old sister Becca (that's short for Rebecca) and my baby brother Squirt. No, his real name's not Squirt, it's John Philip Ramsey, Jr. But when he was born, he was the tiniest baby in the hospital, so the nurses gave him a special nickname.

As I said, my family and I live in Stoney-brook, Connecticut, but we used to live in Oakley, New Jersey, and that was great because my grandparents lived on the same street as we did and so did a lot of my aunts and uncles and cousins. One of my cousins, Keisha, was my very best friend. She and I have the exact same birthday, and Keisha always seemed to know what I was feeling about things.

I'd lived in Oakley since I was a baby, but then Daddy's company transferred him to Stamford, Connecticut, so we found this house in Stoneybrook, nearby. I'll tell you honestly, sometimes I still miss Oakley. It was a little easier to be myself there. And I especially miss Keisha. I mean, how many best friends have known each other since they were one day old?

Well, Stoneybrook doesn't have Keisha. And it doesn't have my wonderful grandparents or my aunts and uncles. But it does offer a lot of other things. Since we moved here, I enrolled in a very good ballet school in Stamford. To get in, I had to audition. And then Daddy built me my very own ballet barre and practice area in our basement. I also found myself another best friend. Her name is Mallory Pike. And because of Mallory, I now belong to one of the greatest clubs in the world —

3

the Baby-sitters Club. Maybe that's been the best thing about moving to Stoneybrook.

The club was the great idea of Kristy Thomas. She's an eighth-grader who goes to my school. Last year, when she was in seventh grade, she got together with a bunch of friends who love to baby-sit and they formed a club. They sent out fliers to all the families in the neighborhood — very professional — and pretty soon they had a booming business. Leave it to Kristy. She's a take-charge type of person. The club meets three afternoons a week — Monday, Wednesday, and Friday from 5:30 until 6:00 — and families who need a baby-sitter know to call us up during club hours. The great thing is that one of us is bound to be free. So our clients are sure of getting a sitter and, meanwhile, we get plenty of jobs. *Everybody's* happy!

All the club members are eighth-graders except for Mallory and me. Mallory got in because all the Baby-sitters knew her. See, the girls had sat a lot for Mallory's family, the Pikes. Oh, I guess I forgot to tell you. Mallory is from a big family, and I'm talking *big*. Believe it or not, there are eight kids in the Pike family. Mallory's the oldest. Mrs. Pike used to hire sitters from the club and Mallory would always help them out. Of course, being the oldest of eight, Mallory was always great with the kids. So when there was an opening in the club, Kristy decided to let her in. Lucky me, she decided to let me in at the same time!

How did I get started on all this? Wasn't I telling you about Becca and the TV show? Well, to get back to the beginning of the story, there I was in the kitchen with Mama, Daddy, and Squirt. And there was Becca in the living room, bellowing at us with the full power of her lungs. Mama looked at Daddy.

"Do you think someone wants our attention?" she said, and laughed.

"You guys!" Becca was now standing in the kitchen doorway. Her arms were crossed over her chest and she had this expression on her face that said, I can't believe you guys are just *standing* there when the best show on TV has come on.

"ABADA!" said Squirt. (He loves to be in on any conversation.)

"Okay, everybody!" Becca said. "If you hurry, you won't miss anything."

Mama lifted Squirt out of his high chair and wiped his face clean with the washcloth we keep in the kitchen for that purpose.

"So what is this five-star show we're missing?" Daddy asked.

"*P.S. 162,*" I explained. "Becca says all the

5

kids in her class watch it every Friday night. I think Becca has a crush on one of the kids in it."

"I do not!" Becca cried. She was already back in the living room and settled in her seat. Mama followed her and set Squirt on the carpet. Then she and Daddy squeezed onto the couch next to Becca. I laid down on the floor on my back and lifted one of my legs toward me to stretch it out. Sometimes when I watch TV, I use the time to do stretching exercises. I've got my family trained. They're completely used to seeing me sprawled all over the floor like a contortionist. Becca's the only one who ever complains, and that's only if I block her view of the screen.

"Where's the popcorn?" Daddy joked, as we all settled down for the show.

"Shh!" Becca said. Her eyes were glued to the TV, even though all that was on was a commercial for toothpaste.

I'd seen this show, *P.S. 162*, a couple of times before, and I'd liked it okay. But until that day I'd never thought it was anything special. It's about an inner city elementary school, and the class includes all different kinds of kids. The character Becca has a crush on is named Lamont. He's black, and in the show he's the most popular kid in the class. For good reason, too — Lamont is smart, funny, *and* good-looking. In the class, there're also Latin kids, Asian kids, and white kids. One of the white characters is named Waldo, and I've got to admit, he always makes me laugh. He's got weird, spiky hair and he wears this pair of thick black glasses and he's an incredible science whiz. You know, one of those kids who lives and breathes science, but put him in the real world and he can barely tie his shoes. When he talks to the other kids, he always uses big, science-y words like "zygotes" and "ecosystem," and of course the other kids don't have a *clue* what he's talking about.

That night, finally — after what seemed like about a hundred commercials — the show came on. In the opening scene, as a joke, one of the kids swiped Lamont's homework and Lamont was looking for it everywhere. Class was about to begin. The teacher rapped on her desk to get everyone's attention and then asked for a volunteer to write the homework on the board. She stared at Lamont. He slunk low in his desk chair, trying to avoid her gaze.

"Lamont," the teacher said.

From her seat on the couch, Becca let out a

long, low wail. "Oh, no!" she cried. You would've thought *Becca* was the one caught without her homework.

Daddy started to laugh.

"I take it Lamont is the boy Becca's got a crush on," he teased.

"Shhh!" Becca said.

Just then in the show Waldo raised his hand.

"Miss Pedagogue," he said, very seriously. "I've got the correct answer. Allow me."

He strode up to the board and wrote the word "fission" in big block letters. The teacher groaned and buried her head in her hands.

"Waldo," she said, "I hate to break it to you, but this is history class. After history comes English. And *then*, after English, comes science. How about if you just hang onto your answer for a couple more periods? Believe me, when it's science, I'll let you know."

Waldo got flustered and dropped the magnifying glass that he keeps in his pocket onto the floor. All the other kids in the class laughed. So did the voices on the laugh track.

When that scene was over, *P.S. 162* faded off for a commercial break and an ad for some gasoline company came on.

Becca stared dreamily at the screen.

"Isn't Lamont the cutest guy in the world?" she said with a sigh.

8

"He's pretty nice, all right," Mama agreed.

"I think Waldo's funnier," I said.

"You like *Waldo*?" Becca said. "So does everyone in my class. Charlotte Johanssen said that the kid who plays him used to go to Stoneybrook Elementary School." (Charlotte Johanssen is Becca's best friend. She's lived in Stoneybrook a lot longer than we have.)

"Is that true?" asked Mama.

"Cross my heart," said Becca. She traced an X on her chest over her heart. Then she spit on her finger and raised her hand in a sort of oath. I still didn't know whether to believe her. "Charlotte said he always used to get his picture in the paper here. But now he lives in L.P."

"L.A." I corrected her. "Los Angeles — in California."

Hmm. Well, maybe Becca *was* telling the truth. She certainly seemed to have enough details.

"The kids in my class only like the show because of Waldo," Becca went on. "But not me," she said, pouting. "I wish *Lamont* was the one who'd gone to Stoneybrook Elementary."

I was curious to find out more about this Waldo business, but it was too late to ask Becca any more questions. The commercials had finished up and the show had come back on. Lamont was back on screen, cornering the kid who had swiped his homework.

"Quiet!" Becca said.

Squirt toddled over and crawled onto my stomach. I picked him up, sat up, and plunked my little brother onto my lap. I stared at the screen and waited for Waldo to come back on. This new information made the show a lot more interesting. I tried to picture Waldo playing baseball with the kids in the schoolyard here. Or shopping for school clothes at Washington Mall. Maybe he got those weird glasses of his at the same place Mallory got her glasses.

When the show was over I ran to the telephone to call Mallory. I figured if there was any family that would know about this Waldo business, it would have to be the Pikes. I mean, out of eight kids, somebody's got to know something. That's one advantage to having a best friend from such a large family. It's like calling Information Central.

When Mallory came to the phone, she confirmed everything Becca had said.

Yes, it was true. Waldo and his family did live in Stoneybrook, only not full-time anymore. She said that Waldo's real name is Derek Masters, and she told me that now that he had to be out in California for a chunk of the year, his family had moved with him to L.A. They would be back when he had finished taping *P.S. 162*.

"How do you know all this?" I asked.

"A *star* from *Stoneybrook*? Are you kidding? It's big news. Everybody knows it," said Mallory. "Anyway, Derek used to be in Nicky's class." Nicky is one of Mallory's younger brothers. He's eight years old and in the third grade.

"In Nicky's class!?" I practically shrieked. Uh-oh. I was getting star struck, and by the time this whole mess was over, I was not going to be the only one. "Put Nicky on the phone, will you?" I asked.

When Nicky got on, he told me all about Derek. He told me that Derek had been a local child model, that he'd been in a lot of magazine ads and even on one TV commercial here. Somehow, that had all led to the job on *P.S. 162*.

"Wow!" I said. I couldn't believe that no one had told me any of this before. This was hot news, and I wanted a chance to talk about it with my friends. I couldn't wait for the next meeting of the Baby-sitters Club.

CHAPTER 2

By the time I skidded into the meeting on Monday, everybody else was already there. Kristy Thomas (remember, I told you she's the one who started the club) was sitting in her director's chair, wearing her visor, as usual. As I walked in that day, she was chewing on the tip of a pencil, waiting for Claudia's digital clock to turn to 5:30 so she could start the meeting. When I caught sight of her, I almost giggled. To me, it kind of looked like she was gnawing on a cigar. The way Kristy sits in that room and takes over, you'd think it was *her* house, *her* bedroom and *her* director's chair. That's because she's the club president, but actually we hold the meetings in Claudia Kishi's house. Claudia is our vice-president. She has her own bedroom with her own phone and private phone number, and she's nice enough to let us use them for the club.

I should probably tell you a little bit about

the club members so you know who we are. There're six of us all together. I'll start right at the top.

Kristy? Well, she's . . . Kristy. Sometimes people think she's a little bossy, but she certainly does know how to take charge of the club, and I really admire her for that. Kristy's a tomboy type. She's short for her age and she's got brown hair and brown eyes. She always wears jeans, a turtleneck, a sweater, and sneakers. I think I'd faint if I ever saw her in a dress.

Kristy lives with her mom and Nannie (her grandmother), her three brothers, her stepfather (Watson) and her newly adopted little sister, Emily Michelle. Watson has two other kids from when he was married before, and sometimes they come to stay at the house, too. I call it a house, but I'll tell you what it really is — a mansion. No kidding. See, Watson is a millionaire. And when Kristy's mom married him last year, Kristy and her brothers moved over to the ritzy side of town. Kristy still goes to our school, but she does live a little far away from the rest of us. So we pay her brother Charlie to give her a ride to Claudia's house every time we have a meeting.

Claudia is about as different from Kristy as you can get. I'm talking sun and moon. Clau-

13

dia is Japanese-American and she's got long, sleek, black hair that she has fixed a different way every time I see her. You wouldn't think there could be so many ways to fix hair. That Monday, for instance, she had two French braids pulled back and wound into one. She's also a wild dresser. At that meeting she was wearing a bright pink T-shirt, a short red flouncy skirt, and underneath the skirt she had on black footless tights that she had rolled up to mid-calf.

Claudia has a little bit of trouble in school, but what she's really good at is art. That's probably why she gets such interesting ideas for putting wild and colorful clothes together. She loves to paint and sculpt and make collages, and her room is cluttered with the boxes she keeps all her materials in. She's got boxes of paints, boxes of brushes, and boxes of fabric scraps, interesting bits of paper, ribbon, wood pieces, everything. You name it, Claudia can turn it into art.

The only boxes in her room that aren't filled with art supplies are the ones stuffed with junk food. You might not think someone so into art would be into Cheez Doodles and Tastee Cakes, but Claudia is. She keeps a stash in her room and passes it around at all our meetings.

The secretary of our club is Mary Anne Spier. Mary Anne is short, like Kristy, and also has brown hair and brown eyes. Sometimes Mary Anne can be on the quiet side, and she's very sensitive (also romantic), but she's extremely organized, and that's exactly what makes her perfect to be club secretary. Mary Anne's job is to schedule all the baby-sitting appointments as they come in. She has to keep track of everyone's schedule, so she always knows who's free when, and believe me, that's a lot to juggle. Take me, for instance. I probably have the busiest schedule of anyone in the club, what with my ballet classes and a semiregular sitting job. Keeping track of me alone is practically a full-time job.

Mary Anne's mother died when she was a baby, so she lives alone with her father. Mr. Spier can be kind of strict, but in the past year he's loosened up a lot. Now Mary Anne even has a boyfriend! His name is Logan Bruno and he's very nice. Can you believe it? The shyest girl is the one who gets the steady boyfriend? And to top it off, she's the only club member who has one!

The last important officer is our treasurer, and that's Dawn Schafer. Dawn has long, white-blonde hair and she's a real California girl. Her whole family used to live in southern

California, but then her parents got divorced. Now her father lives there with her brother, and Dawn lives here with her mother in an old, restored farmhouse.

Dawn's an independent type. She has her own opinions and she does what she likes. For instance, she won't have anything to do with Claudia's junk food. Dawn's strictly a natural-foods girl. Her idea of a good sandwich is tofu, sprouts, and tahini on whole wheat pita bread. Try offering that to Claudia.

Those four are the eighth-grade members of the club. Then there's Mallory and me, the lowly sixth-graders. We are the junior officers. We came into the club when one of the other girls, Stacey McGill, moved back to New York City. (My family moved right into her old house!) Since we're younger, we mostly take jobs in the afternoons or weekends. The only night jobs we're allowed to take are with our own families.

You know pretty much about me already, and you know that Mallory is one of eight Pike kids, so I'll just add that Mallory loves to read and that sometimes she even writes and illustrates her own stories. She has glasses and braces (which she hates), and pierced ears (which she loves), and she's just about the best friend I could have hoped for when I moved to Stoneybrook.

I think that's all you need to know about the club members. Oh, yeah. I almost forgot. We also have two associate members, Shannon Kilbourne and Logan Bruno. (Logan's not *just* Mary Anne's boyfriend. He's also a great baby-sitter.) We call our associates to help us out if we get too many jobs to handle ourselves. Logan and Shannon don't come to the meetings or anything. They're kind of like our standby crew.

Anyway, I was telling you about that Monday's meeting, wasn't I? When I slipped into Claudia's room that afternoon, I found a place on the floor next to Mallory. Kristy waved that pencil of hers through the air like a baton.

"This meeting will now come to order," she said.

I always sit up straighter when Kristy starts a meeting.

"Any business?" she asked.

"Dues are due." Dawn smiled.

We all groaned. Really, none of us minds paying dues. The money goes for things we need, like Kid-Kits, which are these neat boxes of toys and games we sometimes bring on jobs with us. I think we just like to groan every week because it's fun.

"All right, all right," Kristy cut us off. "Any other club business?" she asked, after Dawn had collected our money.

"Anyone want M & M's?" Claudia asked. She fished a bag of candy out from under her bed and passed it around.

Kristy heaved a loud sigh. She doesn't consider Claudia's snacks to be "club business." (But I notice that she always takes something when the bag comes around.)

Of course, I was *dying* to bring up the matter of Waldo, but I knew that if Kristy didn't consider snacks to be official enough business, she'd hardly approve of my bringing up Waldo. I knew that I'd have to wait until the end of the meeting for that.

Kristy flipped through the club notebook. We use the notebook to write down all the important things that happen on our jobs — things about the kids, the families, anything the other sitters should know. Then, once a week, we're supposed to read what everyone else wrote. That's Kristy's way of keeping us all informed.

I was still thinking about Waldo when the first couple of calls came in. Mary Anne scheduled some sitters. The phone rang a third time. Kristy took the call.

"Oh, hello, Mrs. Masters," she said. "Yes,

I've heard of your family. . . . You're back in town? . . . Sure. . . . Sure. . . . We'd be delighted to sit for your boys."

Mallory nudged me and grinned. I shot her a questioning look. I hadn't recognized the name.

Kristy hung up and gave us the news. Someone named Mrs. Masters was looking for an afternoon sitter for her two boys, Derek and Todd.

"Derek!" Now I got it. "Derek! You mean Waldo? Are you saying that that was Waldo's mother calling us for a *baby-sitter?*"

Kristy shot me a look that said, Calm down, Jessi, this is a baby-sitting job, not a meeting of the Derek Masters Fan Club.

Mary Anne checked the appointment book.

"Someone for Wednesday?" she asked. "Well, it looks like the only one who's free is Jessi."

Often on Wednesdays I sit for a family called the Braddocks, but the other club members had started to take over some of those jobs. That had left me with a little more free time.

"Me?" I squeaked. "You want to send me to baby-sit for Waldo?"

"Derek," Kristy corrected me. "Derek and his four-year-old brother, Todd. Anyway, that would work out well, Jessi. The Masterses live only two blocks away from you."

"They do?" I cried. How come I didn't know anything about that? I guess I thought the house should have a big neon star on top of it. Or Waldo's handprints pressed into the sidewalk outside, like at that famous Hollywood theater.

Well, this was more than I had bargained for. When I came to the meeting, I had only wanted to *talk* about Waldo. Now it turned out I was going to be baby-sitting for him.

Kristy called back Mrs. Masters and told her to expect me on Wednesday afternoon.

As you can see, things were already going awfully fast. That's what happens when you get involved with show biz.

CHAPTER 3

The thing about my life is that my schedule is so crazy, I don't have time to dwell on any one thing for very long. After the meeting that day I rushed back to my house to dinner and homework. Then, the next day, right after school, I had dance class. . . . Or, as Mme Noelle would say, "donce closs."

Mme Noelle is my ballet teacher and she's perfect for the role. I can't imagine her doing anything else. She's an older woman, and she teaches class in a leotard and a long rehearsal skirt. Instead of wearing ballet slippers she wears dance shoes with heels on them. Apparently, she was quite a beautiful ballerina in her time. You can still see it in the graceful way she moves her arms, and in her carriage in general. (I love that word "carriage." And I don't mean the horse-drawn kind. I mean the way she walks and moves and carries herself.)

"Modemoiselle Romsey, point thot toe."

That was Mme Noelle. Did I forget to tell you that she's a stern taskmaster? Well, she is. When you're there in class doing the exercises, she watches your every move.

"Modemoiselle Romsey, turn out the stonding thigh, if you please. Lead with your heel, and drop thot hip."

There's no escaping the watchful eye of Mme Noelle. Now, the crazy thing about dance class is that part of you doesn't want a teacher to be scrutinizing you and giving you a zillion corrections, but then again, part of you does. When a teacher pays attention to you, it means she thinks your work in class is *worth* paying atttention to. And, of course, the only way you get better is to find out what you're doing wrong.

"Modemoiselle Romsey, *drop* that hip!"

(I know what I just said, but when I'm in class, sometimes it's hard to remember why it is I like corrections.)

That day in class it seemed to take forever for my body to warm up and start to move the way it should. We started class with exercises at the barre and I just felt a little off. Then we moved into the room for what we call center work. We always start off slowly and work up to big leaps and things like that.

Usually I like to stand in the front of class so I can correct myself from what I see in the mirror. But that day, Mme Noelle had already bombarded me with so many corrections that I decided to stay toward the back. It didn't matter, though. Mme Noelle saw me anyway.

"Modemoiselle Romsey! How many times do I have to say? Straighten thot back leg!"

Oh, my head was swimming. In ballet, sometimes there're just too many things to remember at once.

I was starting to feel a little discouraged toward the end of class, but then, when we lined up in the corner to do the final leaps across the floor, the man who accompanies us on the piano struck up a really different and wonderful piece of music. Usually he plays a lot of classical themes, which I do enjoy, but all of a sudden he switched to a lively waltz from an old Broadway show. I looked at Katie Beth, one of my friends in the class, and we both grinned.

Mme Noelle walked us through a series of steps and then we did them to the music. Something about that music gave me energy. The footwork Madame had given us was fast, and when it was my turn my feet practically flew and I felt myself soar into the air. I caught a quick glimpse of my reflection in the mirror while I was at the height of my leap. Good grief! I looked like . . . like a ballerina! I mean, I know that's what I'm supposed to be, but it really feels super when all the hard work comes together.

This may sound corny, but every once in awhile in class my overwhelming love for ballet just comes flooding into me. Nothing else gives me so much pleasure. And no other art form seems as beautiful or as moving.

When the class ended we all applauded Mme Noelle. She bowed her head graciously as she always does and then held up one hand to get our attention. She had an announcement to make.

"*Mes petites,*" she said. (That's what she calls us. It's French for "my little girls.") "I want to advise you thot the Stoneybrook Civic Center will be holding aw-di-see-ons for *Swan Lake.*" (Did you get that? She meant auditions.) "The aw-di-see-ons, as I understond it, are Soturday next. Those girls who feel ready might be brave to try out."

Auditions for *Swan Lake*! At the Stoneybrook Civic Center! That was really something. *Swan Lake* is a ballet about an enchanted swan, and it's one of the most beautiful ballets ever choreographed. And now it was going to be performed at the Stoneybrook Civic Center, which is a wonderful theater. The theater's not in New York City, but it's so good that it might as well be. A lot of famous stars you would have heard of are always performing there.

I sat down on the floor to unlace my toe shoes. I was thinking that someday I'll be good enough to audition for a ballet like that. Maybe a few years from now. Three years, two . . . if I were lucky. Who could tell? Maybe even next year. I picked up my dance bag and started to head for the dressing room.

"Modemoiselle Romsey." Mme Noelle caught me just as I was almost out the door. Oh, no. My heart sank. Was she going to give me one last correction? Just when I had been able to end the class on such a good note. I braced myself to hear what she had to say.

"*Ma petite*, do you think you might aw-di-see-on for *Swan Lake*?" she asked.

"Me?" My voice came out in a high-pitched squeak. "Well, I don't think this year. Maybe I'll be ready next year. I mean — "

"You're a gifted doncer," Madame cut me off. "This production will be quite professional. It would be a wonderful experience for you. Broadening. I do hope you consider, dear." She handed me a flier with the information. Then Madame smiled at me and gestured for me to go ahead of her out the door.

"Thank you, Madame," I managed to sputter.

I glanced at the flier. It said that there would be three audition calls altogether, with eliminations after each one. As I walked to the dressing room, my thoughts were flying. Mme Noelle had singled me out to encourage me to audition. Maybe I actually should try out.

In the dressing room the other girls were all talking about Madame's news.

"The Stoneybrook Civic Center!" said one. "You know, the productions in that theater get reviewed by the papers in New York City."

"I bet a lot of dancers from New York will come out for the auditions," said another. "I bet the competition will be really stiff."

"Yeah, like *A Chorus Line*."

"Oh, no!" groaned Katie Beth.

Katie Beth was still wearing her toe shoes. She leaped to the center of the dressing room floor and began turning pirouettes as fast as she could.

"Do I get the part? Do I get the part?" she called out.

After her last pirouette, she struck a pose from the ballet, nuzzling her cheek against her shoulder as a swan might do to preen its feathers.

We all applauded.

"Encore!" we shouted. "Encore!" Katie Beth collapsed on the floor, breathless and panting.

"No way," she said, laughing. "I guess I'm no enchanted swan. All I am is a tired ballet student."

After I had changed, I stuffed my sweaty tights and leotard into my bag. Then I slung the bag over my shoulders and waved to my friends.

"Do you think you'll try out?" asked Katie Beth, as we left school.

"Maybe," I said. "I don't know." That was true. I didn't.

Outside the school, Mama was waiting for me in the car. Becca and Squirt were with her. I slid into the backseat next to Squirt. He grabbed my cheek and gave me a spitty kiss.

"How was class?" Mama asked.

"Good," I said. I told her about the auditions for *Swan Lake*. I told her that Mme Noelle had drawn me aside at the end of class to encourage me to try out.

"That's wonderful, honey," Mama said. I could see her smiling in the rearview mirror.

"It is," I replied with a sigh, "but I don't know. Maybe it's *too* professional for me right now. I mean, how can I compete with dancers from New York? I mean, do I even *want* to?"

"It's up to you," Mama said. "It does sound

like an opportunity. You might want to go ahead and go to the audition even if it is scary. But that's your decision, Jessi. You just let me know."

Parents. Doesn't it seem backwards that they always want to make decisions for you when you *don't* want them to? Like, "No, you can't stay out past 9 PM,'" or "No, you can't get your ears pierced." But when you actually *might* want them to go ahead and *tell* you what to do, what do they say? "It's up to you. You just let me know."

Mom pulled the car into traffic and turned on the radio.

I stared out the window. I pictured myself onstage in a swan costume. I couldn't be Odette, of course. Odette is the queen of the swans and the star of the ballet. But maybe I could be one of the swan maidens who dance in the corps. In my fantasy I did quick turns across the stage. I was a graceful, mysterious swan escaping from hunters.

Okay. The fantasy did it. I was hooked. Yes, I did want to be in *Swan Lake*. More than anything, in fact. Right then and there I decided to try out. Yes, I'd go to the audition, all right. I would *do* it.

CHAPTER 4

Before I knew it, it was Wednesday afternoon, and time for me to baby-sit for DEREK MASTERS! and his little brother, Todd. If you think I was excited, you should've seen Becca. When I was getting ready to leave, she followed me to our front door, firing questions at me all the way.

"Ask him if he knows Lamont. I mean, of course he knows Lamont. Ask him if Lamont's as nice as he is on TV. Ask him what kind of games Lamont likes to play. Ask him . . . ask him what Lamont likes to eat for breakfast."

Honestly.

"Becca, I'm baby-sitting for Waldo, not for Lamont." I heaved a big sigh. "Look. Now you've got *me* all confused. I mean, I'm baby-sitting for *Derek*. Anyway, I thought you said you didn't have a crush on Lamont."

"I don't!" Becca said hotly. "I'm just curious, that's all."

"Sounds like a pretty serious crush to me," I said.

Becca whirled around in a huff and stomped off to her room. I grabbed my sweater and was out the door.

Well, Becca may have been a bit over the edge about Lamont, but to tell you the truth, I was not much calmer about Derek. As I walked down the street to the Masterses' house, my heart started racing. I was going to meet a real *TV* star! Every week people all over the country watched *P.S. 162* and every week they laughed at Waldo and his silly science. Hmm. It suddenly occured to me that maybe Derek would be able to help me with my science homework. (I *had* been having a little bit of trouble with it lately.) At any rate, this would be a good opportunity to get his autograph. If I wanted to be clever, I could even get him to autograph my science book!

I stood at the front door of the Masterses' and brought my finger up to the doorbell. I took a deep breath and swallowed hard. This was as bad as an audition. I certainly had as many butterflies in my stomach.

"Go *on*," I said to myself. Sometimes I have to take myself in hand and tell myself what to do. "Just go ahead. Ring that bell."

B-R-R-R-R-I-I-I-I-N-G!

I jumped at the sound of the bell. The door opened and a nice-looking woman stood there smiling. Behind her were two boys.

I looked past them into the house. I was looking for Derek, for a boy wearing thick, horn-rimmed glasses.

"Hello," the woman said cheerfully. She extended her hand to shake mine. "You must be Jessi. I'm Mrs. Masters, and, come here, boys." She beckoned to the two children behind her. "This is Todd," she said, putting her hand on the little one's shoulder. "And this is Derek."

"Derek?" I don't think I hid my surprise. The boy she introduced as Derek was just a regular-looking kid. Where were the glasses? And what about his spiky hair?

"I look different from on the show, huh?" Derek said. I guess my mouth was still hanging open.

"No glasses," I managed to say.

"Waldo wears the glasses," said Derek. "I have 20-20 vision."

Mrs. Masters ushered me into the house and started showing me around. Well, the famous Derek Masters was not only regular-looking himself, he also lived in a perfectly regular house. In fact, it was kind of messy. There were newspapers all over the floor in the living room and dishes piled up high in the kitchen sink. What had I expected? A Hollywood set?

Mrs. Masters showed me where she kept the emergency numbers and then she set out a snack for the boys and me in the kitchen. She was just going to be gone a couple of hours, so she said good-bye to Todd and Derek and left me there in charge.

"Well," I said to the boys. They looked up at me over their glasses of juice. "Tell me about L.A. What's the TV business like, Derek?"

"Yuk," Derek said. "Work. Actually, I like it okay, but I'm glad we're on a break."

"*P.S. 162* feels like work?" I said. "Gee, it looks like so much fun on TV."

"It can be fun," Derek said, "but it's long hours."

"Then when do you go to school?" I asked.

"I have a private tutor there," said Derek. "He works with me on breaks between tapings, whenever we can fit it in." Derek stuffed a whole fig cookie into his mouth. "I'm starting school here again next Monday," he grinned. The words were all garbled with cookie. Derek was a regular kid, all right.

I wished I had taped our conversation that afternoon. It probably sounded pretty comical. For awhile, I didn't give up trying to ask Derek questions about the show — what it was like being a TV star and all. But, every chance he could, Derek changed the subject and asked me things about Stoneybrook. Did I know anything about Stoneybrook Elementary School? he wanted to know. Were the same teachers still there? Did I know if any of the same kids would be in his class?

Of course, I know plenty about Stoneybrook Elementary. Becca goes there and so do just about all the kids I baby-sit for.

"Do you know Nicky Pike?" I asked.

Derek's face lit up. "Nicky's a great guy."

As Derek talked on, the light bulb finally flashed in my brain. Derek wasn't interested in talking about show biz. Here was a kid who'd been away from his class for almost a year, and he was just worried about how he would fit in when he went back.

"I hope the kids don't think I've changed," he said, "or treat me differently. Some people act pretty strange about this star stuff."

"Really?" I gulped. I was glad Derek didn't know how silly *I* had gotten.

After the boys had finished their snack, Derek brought me up to his room. He pulled an old, battered box out from one of his drawers. It was a game of Candy Land.

"Landy Cand!" he said to Todd. "You want to play Landy Cand?" Then he explained to me, "That's what Todd used to call it when he was two."

See, not only was Derek a regular kid, he was also a regular, everyday brother.

The three of us settled on Derek's floor for a game. And another. And another. Whenever Todd got a card with candy on it, he brought it up to his mouth and pretended to eat it with loud munching sounds. Derek let Todd win every other game.

When we were about Candy Land-ed out, Derek folded up the board and put the game away. I spotted another box in the drawer. On the top was a large photo of Derek.

"What's this?" I asked curiously. I picked up the photo. It was of Derek's face, but it was blown up and it looked like some kind of fancy movie star photo. His hair looked kind of windswept, but in a perfectly styled kind of way. His smile was big and toothpaste-y. At the bottom of the photo his name was printed in big letters. Derek looked embarrassed that I had found it.

"There's more," I said. The whole box was filled with copies of the photo.

"It's my head shot," Derek said shyly.

"Your what?" I asked.

"Head shot," Derek repeated. "If you're an actor, you get a fancy picture taken of you like this and then you send it around to all the people who might give you work."

"Really?" I said. It seemed so . . . so, I don't know. . . . So professional.

"Yeah," said Derek. "You take them to auditions with you and stuff."

"Auditions," I mumbled. I wondered if dancers were supposed to have photos, too.

"I'm going on an audition soon," I told Derek. Even as I said the word, my stomach started knotting up. I may have decided to go ahead with the audition, but I was obviously still more than a little scared.

"Really?" said Derek. Now it was his turn to be surprised. "What kind of audition? An acting thing?"

"Sort of," I said. "For a ballet."

I explained to Derek about my dance classes and about this Stoneybook Civic Center production of *Swan Lake*. I told him that Mme Noelle had encouraged me to try out.

"Great!" said Derek. "I know all about auditions. I'll be your coach. I'll tell you exactly how to land this job."

Derek didn't have time to do any coaching that day, though. Downstairs, the front door banged open.

"I'm home!" Mrs. Masters called.

Derek came downstairs with me. "Thanks

for all the news about Stoneybrook Elementary," he said.

"Sure," I replied. "And don't worry. You'll do fine. Hey, especially in science," I suggested, trying to be helpful. "You could make friends just by doing everybody's science homework."

"Science!" Derek shook his head as if he were going crazy. "I hate science!" he exclaimed. "I get F's!"

"You do?" I said. I couldn't help laughing.

Derek narrowed his eyes, pretending to be mad.

"I know, I know. I'm confusing you with Waldo. I'm going to have to start a list. On one side I'll put all the things Waldo does. On the other side I'll put the things Derek does."

Mrs. Masters paid me and I said good-bye to the boys. I hurried down the street and headed for my afternoon Baby-sitters Club meeting at Claudia's house. I couldn't wait to tell my friends all about Derek and what a nice kid he was. And wait'll Becca hears, I thought.

Uh-oh. I stopped short. Becca! I'd completely forgotten to ask Derek anything about Lamont! Oh, well. I sighed as I thought of how mad Becca would get. I ran the rest of the way to the meeting.

CHAPTER 5

Sunday

How about this for an idea? A new TV series called <u>Baby-sitter for the Stars.</u> I got the idea yesterday when I was sitting for Nicky and the triplets. Jessi came over with the kids <u>she</u> was sitting for, and guess who she brought... the one and only <u>DEREK MASTERS</u>! Things started out pretty well, but then, I'm not sure what happened. Something just went very, very wrong.

You can tell from what Mallory wrote in the club notebook that she had caught DEREK MASTERS! fever. That's the way it seemed to go. Just when one person would be getting over it, another person would catch it. It was contagious.

Anyway, that Saturday, things did get a little strained. Who knows, maybe it was all my fault. Maybe I shouldn't have tried to get everybody together in the first place. But Becca started it. And Mallory pushed it. And then the triplets made it worse.

Come to think of it, Derek didn't help the situation any himself.

See, this is how it started. I was still home, getting ready to go over to the Masterses' house for another afternoon baby-sitting job. Becca followed me to the door while I was putting on my jacket. She was begging, I mean absolutely *begging* me to take her along.

"Please, please, please, please, *please*," she said.

"Becca," I said, "you know I can't take you with me on a job."

"But Derek is probably lonely," she whined. "He probably doesn't have any kids here to play with yet. In L.P. he probably gets to play with Lamont all the time."

I rolled my eyes. This time I didn't even bother to correct Becca. She hurried on.

"Does Derek ever say anything about Lamont?" she asked. "I mean, did he ever maybe say anything about how Lamont really loves rock collections?"

What a question. That's my sister, though. You can guess who has her very own rock collection. Miss Rebecca Ramsey, herself.

"Please," Becca started up again.

Okay, Becca was being a little bit of a pest. But as she was talking, I started thinking. It was true, Derek had seemed a little lonely. Practically all he'd talked to me about was whether he was going to be able to make friends at school again. And it just so happened that he and Becca were the same age. I decided that I would ask Derek and his mom if they'd mind if Becca came over to play for awhile. Of course, I wasn't about to tell that to Becca. I figured I'd wait and see what they said first.

"That would be fine with me." Mrs. Masters smiled when I asked her the question. "Derek, what do you think?"

Derek squinted his eyes.

"How old did you say your sister is?" he asked.

"Eight," I said.

Derek's face brightened.

"Eight?" he repeated. "Yeah, sure. Call her up. Tell her to come over."

You should've heard Becca squeal on the other end of the phone. I had to hold the receiver about a mile away from my ear.

Mrs. Masters left us sandwich fixings for lunch, and since it was a nice day, the boys and I decided to have a picnic in the backyard. By the time Becca arrived, Derek was munching on an apple and Todd was trying to spread a big glob of peanut butter onto his bread. I introduced Becca to the boys.

I noticed Becca staring hard at Derek. I had warned her ahead of time that in real life he doesn't have spiky hair and glasses, but I think it still came as a shock.

"Hi," Derek said. "Want an apple?"

Phew, I thought, this is going to go just fine.

Derek asked Becca all kinds of questions about what had been happening in the third grade. Becca, of course, knew lots more than I had been able to tell him. She knew all of the kid stuff, like how one boy had thrown a spitball and been sent to the principal's office, and how a bird had flown through an open auditorium window during the last assembly.

"Really?" said Derek. "Cool."

There was a lull in the conversation. I could

see Becca gearing up to ask her question.

"So, Derek," she said. "What's it like to work with stars?"

"It's okay," said Derek. Suddenly, all the life had drained out of his voice.

"Well, what's it like to work with Lamont? What's he like?"

"He's okay," Derek replied flatly.

"Is he as funny as he is on TV?"

"Yeah, he's funny."

"Is he smart?"

"Pretty smart."

"Do you think he likes rock collections?"

Derek kneeled on the picnic bench. He took a napkin and wadded it up into a ball. "Can we change the subject please?" he said.

That was my first clue that talk about the show was going to make Derek a little testy.

"Hey," I said quickly, "why don't you guys go climb on the jungle gym? But *carefully*, since you just ate."

Derek hopped off the bench and started for the jungle gym. Becca tagged after him, still firing questions.

As I cleaned up the lunch things I had an idea. Maybe it would be better to get Derek together with a boy. I decided to call Mallory and see if maybe I could bring my kids over to visit hers. I knew that Mallory was at home baby-sitting for Nicky and the triplets (her mother had taken the three younger girls shopping). After all, Derek already knew Nicky, and the two of them were even going to be in the same class. I got Mallory on the phone and asked her what she thought.

"DEREK MASTERS!" she screeched. I was beginning to understand how Derek felt. I mean, Mallory is my best friend and all, but she was getting as carried away as everyone else. I reminded Mal that Derek was just a kid.

"Right," she said, calming down. "I remember what you said at the meeting. He's worried the kids won't like him."

"So how about it? Can I bring Derek and Todd and Becca over?" I asked.

Mallory thought it was a super idea. I wrote Mrs. Masters a note telling her where we would be in case she should come home early. Then I rounded up my gang.

"Field trip!" I called. "What would you think about going over to the Pikes' to play?"

"All right!" the kids exclaimed.

When we got to their house, Nicky opened the door. He looked a little shy when he saw Derek. He shifted his feet and smiled a sheepish grin. Derek looked kind of shy himself.

"Ask them in. Ask them in." Mallory hurried up behind Nicky and swung the door open wide.

"Hello," she said, smiling right at Derek. She stuck out her hand to shake his. "I'm Mallory Pike." She was standing at attention and pronouncing her words strangely, a little too precisely. "And you must be Derek. I'm so pleased that you could come visit us in our home today."

Why was she talking like that? What did she think she was doing? Greeting the Queen of England?

"Mal," I said, trying to cut her off.

"Yes, yes," she went on. "We are very pleased to extend our hospitality, aren't we, Nicky? Do come in."

Nicky smiled another one of his embarrassed smiles.

"Hi, Derek. Uh, how's Hollywood?" he asked.

"It's okay." Derek shrugged.

"*Tsk, tsk, tsk*," Mallory shook her head and clicked her tongue. "Now, Nicky. I'm sure Derek is tired to death of talking about Hollywood and show business." Mallory gave me a little wink, like she was in the know.

I'd never seen Mallory act quite like this. And where was she getting this voice of hers?

She sounded like she was about to recite Shakespeare.

"The other children are out back," she said. Other *children*? Who was she talking about, the triplets or some precious little boys in sailor suits? "Everyone is *so* looking forward to meeting you."

"Mallory," I whispered as we cut through the house to the back door. "This isn't high tea. Why are you talking like this?"

"Am I talking funny?" she whispered back.

"Just a little," I said.

"I guess I'm just nervous. I figured Derek would think we're a bunch of nobodies."

When Nicky opened the back door, Derek spotted the badminton net.

"Badminton!" he said. A big smile stretched across his face. "Great! I love badminton!"

"See," I mouthed to Mallory. "He's a *kid*."

"Right," Mallory mouthed back. "Derek," she said. "Would you care to join the others in a game of — "

I shot Mallory another look. Her face relaxed.

"I mean, do you want to play badminton with the guys?" she asked.

"Sure!" said Derek. "Let's go!"

The triplets, Nicky's brothers, were already at the net. Their names are Adam, Byron, and

Jordon and they're ten years old, two years older than Nicky. Sometimes, because they're older, they can go a little too far with their teasing. They like to lord it over Nicky, and I really don't think they liked the idea of a TV star who was younger than they were. So they took one side of the net and Nicky, Derek, Becca, and Todd positioned themselves on the other.

"We're gonna cream you squirts," said Byron.

Jordan and Adam slammed a high five.

But when Adam served the birdie, Derek jumped to hit it and slammed it right back.

"Whoa," Adam said, taken by surprise. "Think you're cool, huh?"

Well, the game went on like that. Any birdie the triplets served up, Derek managed to hit right back over the net. Derek and his team were winning, and the triplets weren't used to being beaten. Especially not by "squirts."

"Do they teach you that on *P.S. 162*?" Byron jeered.

Oh, no. I couldn't believe this was happening. Why couldn't anyone just act *normal* around Derek? Becca had been hounding him for information, Mal had treated him like royalty, and now the triplets were going to be jealous and nasty about the show. Each person seemed to have a different way of acting creepy, but acting creepy was the general theme.

"Is that what they teach you in star school?" Jordan joined in.

Suddenly, Derek's face turned bright red.

"Forget it," he said. "Just forget it. Who cares about your crummy old game." He threw down his racket and turned to face the triplets. "Anvil Head!" he shouted. "Cactus Brain! Pizza Breath!"

Pizza Breath??? Before I had time to step in and referee, Derek had stomped out of the yard and was calling me after him.

"Come on, Jessi," he said. "I'm going home!"

I grabbed Todd by one hand and Becca by the other.

"Mallory," I said quickly, "I'll talk to you later, I guess."

CHAPTER 6

Did you ever notice that things often get worse before they get better? When we got back to the Masterses' house after the badminton game, I spent a lot of time trying to calm Derek down. But Derek didn't feel like being calmed.

"It'll be worse when I get to school," he complained.

"No, it won't." I tried to shrug the whole thing off. "It was just the game." Derek's face slid into an even deeper sulk. Suddenly, I had a silly thought.

"Hey," I said. "Why do you think they call it *bad*minton?"

Derek cracked a smile. We both started to laugh. It was a giddy laugh, though. That tense kind of laugh that means things really aren't fixed at all.

And believe me, they weren't.

That Monday I had another job at Derek's

house after school. Monday was his first day at Stoneybrook Elementary. Mrs. Masters had had to run off to take care of some legal something or other (handling Derek's career was practically a full-time job for her), and I was waiting at the house with Todd when Derek got home from school.

I was hoping that Derek and I would have time to talk about my upcoming audition. I was still feeling pretty nervous about it, and I thought Derek might be able to give me some tips on how to relax. We never did get a chance to talk about auditions that afternoon, though. What we talked about was Stoneybrook Elementary. When Derek got home, he threw his book bag down on the couch and walked right past me without even saying hello.

"Hi, Derek," I said.

"It was terrible," was his answer.

I got out the snack Mrs. Masters had left and settled the boys around the kitchen table. After a couple of bites of cookie, Derek poured out the whole miserable story.

When he first got to his classroom that morning, he said, the girls circled around him, cooing and mooing like they were sick cows.

"They wouldn't let me through the door," he said. "They all thought they were in love with me."

I nodded my head. I knew what he meant. "Like Becca," I said.

"Worse than Becca," said Derek. "Becca follows me around, but at least she isn't in love with me. I thought those girls might rip my jacket off. You know, so they could keep the pieces for souvenirs."

Derek stuffed another oatmeal cookie in his mouth.

"So I was trying to push my way past them into the class," he said, "but then all of a sudden this flash went off and practically blinded me. Some photographer had shown up at the school, some guy from the *Stoneybrook News*. A reporter was with him. The reporter pushed the girls aside, stuck this stupid tape recorder microphone into my face, and started firing questions at me."

Derek laid his head in his hands.

"The worst part was," he said, "after the reporter was finished, he pushed his notebook into my hands and asked for my autograph."

The *reporter* asked for his *autograph*?

Derek heaved a big sigh.

"What did Mr. Rossi do during all this?" I asked. Mr. Rossi was Derek's teacher. "Didn't he break it up?"

"Break it up?" said Derek. "He made it worse. When the bell rang, he got the reporter out and everybody in their seats. So I thought, Oh good, he's gonna ask us to get out our readers or something like that. But no. The first thing he does is introduce me to the class. He says, 'It's a great honor to welcome back our returning student, that fine boy and wonderful actor, Derek Masters.' "

I couldn't help it. I knew Derek was upset, but I had to giggle. The teacher sounded like some talk show host introducing his next guest.

"It's not funny," Derek said with a groan. "After he introduced me, you know what he made me do?"

"What?" I asked.

"He made me come up to the front of the room and he asked me to give a little talk on my career. 'Tell the class what it's like to work on *P.S. 162*,' he said. 'I'm sure we'd all be interested in hearing how a television show gets produced.' So I had to stand up there and say dopey things, and then I had to answer all the questions the kids had."

I shook my head. It did sound like an awful lot for a first day back.

"One girl asked me if I have to wear makeup on the set and I do, so I said yes. But I should have lied. I should've just said no. You should've heard the boys hooting after that.

The boys don't like me, Jessi. They won't talk to me. They wouldn't play with me on the playground. I knew this was going to happen."

"Just because you said you wear makeup on the set?"

"No, that's not *just* it. When the girls crowded around, the boys called me 'lover boy.' They called me 'spoiled brat.' "

"Brat?" Todd piped in. Poor little Todd sounded horrified. I guess, to a four-year-old, "brat" is about the worst name a person could ever be called.

"Derek, you're not the brat," I said. I shook my head. How come kids can be so mean? Derek just wanted to be one of the guys, but I could see how the boys would be sort of jealous of him. It's not easy to like a kid and think he's a regular guy when reporters are running after him and the girls in the class are practically tearing at his clothes.

"What about Nicky?" I said. "Was Nicky friendly?"

"Oh, yeah," said Derek. "Nicky's real nice. But all of the other boys hate me."

Believe it or not, there was more to the story. As the school day had worn on, the boys had gotten nastier and nastier. One of them had knocked Derek's pencil off his desk when Mr.

Rossi had turned his back. Another boy had squirted him when he walked by the drinking fountain.

"What'd you do then?" I asked.

Derek looked uncomfortable.

"What do you think I should've done?" he asked.

"Well . . ." I paused, "you could just tell them to knock it off."

"I did," said Derek.

"And did they?"

"No, they got worse. What do you think I should do?"

I sat there for a moment, trying to think of a solution to this mess.

"Jessi?" Derek said.

"Yeah?"

"What if I try fighting back? What if I play tricks right back on them?"

"No," I said carefully, "I don't think that's a good idea. No use stooping to their level. That never helps."

"You don't think so?" Derek asked.

I shook my head.

"Jessi," Derek said slowly, "there's one boy in the class who's worse than the rest." I looked at Derek's face. It was all twisted, like he was about to cry. "This kid is really mean to me."

"What's his name?" I asked.

"John," Derek said quickly. "John. When lunch came around, he took my lunch bag and threw it out the window."

"You didn't have lunch?" I cried. No wonder Derek was stuffing cookies into his mouth.

"And during gym, when I wasn't looking, he tied my sneakers together. When I got up, I tripped. Everybody laughed."

"You're kidding!" I exploded. "What a brat! Derek, these kids are calling you a brat and *they* are the biggest brats around. John is . . . is . . ." I couldn't even find the words. "This kid John is a . . . Superbrat!" By this time, I was practically shouting. "I never heard of such a thing. When a new person comes into your class you're supposed to *welcome* him, not tie his shoes together in gym and throw his lunch out the window."

Derek's face was brightening. Now that I had gotten angry, I think it made him feel better, like somebody finally understood what he'd been going through.

"Yeah," he said. "These kids are mean."

Not much later, Derek's mom returned. I stuck around while Derek told her what a horrible day he'd had. Mrs. Masters gathered Todd up and sat him in her lap while Derek went through the story a second time.

I wanted to stay long enough to see if we could put our heads together and come up with some kind of solution. But it was already 5:15. Almost time for the Monday meeting of the Baby-sitters Club. I'd have to hurry to get to Claudia's house on time. On my way there, I noticed that I was walking through the streets much faster than usual. All that anger was really giving me a push. I even got to the meeting a few minutes ahead of time, which for me is really unusual. Everybody was surprised to see me.

"Jessi!" Kristy looked shocked. She checked her watch to make sure she had the right time. "Did my watch slow down? Is it five-thirty already?"

As usual, I plopped onto the floor next to Mallory.

"No," I replied. I was still catching my breath. "But you won't believe what happened to Derek in school today."

My friends were all ears.

"There's a kid in his class," I explained, "a kid who's a real brat. The boy's name is John. But *I* call him Superbrat!"

CHAPTER 7

I swear Jessi's right. It _is_ contagious. Saturday
Everybody wants to get in on the act. I call
it "star fever," and today I had three very bad
cases of it on my hands. The three cases
happened to be named Karen, Hannie,
and Amanda. Well, what else was there
for me to do? I let the girls put on a
play. I mean, all that energy of
theirs had to go _somewhere_. And I
figured it might as well go onstage.

Kristy's afternoon sounded like quite a production. That Saturday she had a job sitting at her own house. Her parents and Nannie were out visiting friends, and her two older brothers were out doing whatever it is that high school brothers do. Karen and Andrew, Kristy's stepsister and stepbrother, were at the house for the weekend, so that left Kristy with Karen, who's six, Andrew, who's four, Kristy's own little brother, David Michael, who's seven, and Emily Michelle, who's two. (She's the little girl who was adopted into Kristy's family.)

When Kristy's parents left, David Michael and Andrew were quietly playing a game of cards and Emily Michelle was taking her afternoon nap. But Karen . . . well, Karen is Karen. That little girl has a wild imagination and more energy than a month-old puppy. You know how puppies just can't help chewing on slippers and shoes and socks and anything else they can get their teeth on? Well, Karen's sort of like that. Only it's not slippers she chews on. It's more like . . . life.

Kristy told me that Karen had started getting a little wild the night before, when the family had sat down together to watch *P.S. 162*. (I guess a lot of families in Stoneybrook had taken to watching the show.) While they were watching, Kristy happened to mention that the actor who played Derek was back in town and that the Baby-sitters Club had lined up a few jobs at his house. Well, that was enough to set Karen's mind spinning. Kristy said that Karen sat there wide-eyed, staring at the TV, amazed that this character on the screen was really a little boy named Derek who actually lived in Stoneybrook.

"You mean he's from *here?*" she sputtered. "But then, but then how did he ever get to be on TV?"

Kristy explained as best she could about actors and how they get jobs.

"Does that mean *I* could be on TV?" This was a whole new revelation for Karen. She jumped up and started reciting all the lines after the actors on TV.

By the time the show was over, Karen's eyes were glazed over. She'd gotten the bug, all right.

"You know, I could do that," she said. "I could be an actor, too. I know how to do what they were doing. It's not so hard. I could be on TV."

That night, Kristy thought the whole thing might blow over. She figured Karen would go to bed and wake up the next morning having forgotten all about this acting business. Well, obviously, Kristy had forgotten who she was dealing with. This, after all, was Karen Brewer, the same Karen who for months and months has sworn that the older woman who lives next door to them is really a witch named Morbidda Destiny. Now, mind you, Karen's had plenty of evidence to the contrary. But will she give up her idea? Not on your life. And she wasn't about to give up this acting idea, either. So she'd had a good night's sleep. So what? That Saturday morning, when Karen woke up, she was ready and eager to start her career. At the breakfast table she made her first move. She asked if Kristy could introduce her to Derek.

Kristy sighed.

"Karen," she said, "Derek is having a very hard time adjusting to being back in Stoney-brook. The last thing he needs right now is people calling him up and asking him favors."

"But he could get me on TV," Karen protested. "I'm sure he could get me on *P.S. 162.*"

"The answer," said Kristy, "is no."

Karen kept pestering Kristy all morning and into the afternoon, and finally Kristy suggested that if Karen wanted to be an actress so badly, maybe she should think of some way to do it herself.

"Okay!" said Karen.

Karen dashed up to the playroom and dug into a big trunk she has there. The trunk is filled with old dress-up clothes. Karen pulled out a big straw hat with a bunch of fake violets on the brim, a pair of long black silken gloves (the kind that go all the way up to your elbows), high-heeled shoes, and a yellow flouncy dress that looks like it had been somebody's prom outfit. She put this odd costume on and walked back down the steps in her tippy shoes.

"Kristy," she called. "I have an idea. Can I call Hannie and Amanda to come over and help me?"

Hannie Papadakis and Amanda Delaney are two little girls who live on Kristy's street. Both of them are good friends with Karen, though the two of them don't get along quite as well.

Kristy took a look at Karen's getup. She felt the edges of her mouth start to twitch into a smile, but she knew she couldn't laugh. That it would hurt Karen's feelings.

"Sure," she said. "Call 'em up." Kristy's used to having a lot of kids around. For her, the more the merrier.

By the time Hannie and Amanda arrived, Karen had already rearranged the living room so it worked better as a stage. She pushed the chairs around so that there was a big empty space at one end of the room, and the chairs became the seats for the audience.

"There!" Karen said, eyeing her work.

Hannie and Amanda stood crammed behind the chairs.

"What are we playing?" asked Hannie.

"Playing!" cried Karen. "This isn't play! This is work!" Karen adjusted the straw hat on her head and hiked up her long yellow gown. "I'm an actress," she announced, as if that explained everything, "and Hannie, you and Amanda can be actresses, too. Of course, I'm the star, though," she added.

"I want to be a star, too," said Amanda.

"Well," Karen paused, "okay."

"If she's a star, I want to be a star," said Hannie.

"*Everybody* can't be stars," Karen protested.

Kristy poked her head in through the door. She'd been listening all along.

"Why not?" she asked.

"*Because*," said Karen. It was as simple as that. "And anyway, Kristy," Karen went on, "you can't come in here yet. We're going to put on a play, but we have to practice it first. You and David Michael and Andrew and Emily Michelle are going to be the audience. The audience isn't *supposed* to see the practice part."

Just then, Kristy heard Emily Michelle stirring upstairs. She had woken up from her nap. Kristy left the girls alone and went upstairs to tend to her new little sister. Karen shut the door to the living room behind her.

Over the course of the next hour or so, Kristy could hear all sorts of commotion coming from Karen's rehearsal.

"No!" she heard Karen shout. "Hannie, you're not supposed to stand *here*. You're supposed to stand *there*."

"But Amanda's standing over there," Hannie said.

"Amanda, weren't you listening? I told you to do a dance with a little twirl and end up on *this* side of the room," Karen directed.

It's always difficult being a director.

When the rehearsal was almost finished, Karen brought her friends up to the playroom and rummaged through the trunk with them, looking for their costumes. Amanda found a black lace dress she wanted to wear.

"No," said Karen. She gave her a red cotton one instead. I think Karen didn't want anyone to be more dressed up than she was. She was, you remember, the star.

The girls ran up and down the stairs several more times, then closed themselves back up in the living room. Kristy could hear Karen's orders and Hannie and Amanda's giggles. Finally, Karen swung open the living room door.

"Come on, everybody!" she cried. "Come on, audience!"

It was time for Karen's production.

Kristy hiked Emily up on her hip and brought David Michael and Andrew into the living room. The "audience" settled themselves into their seats. Karen walked to the center of the stage area and held up her hands for attention.

"Quiet, everybody," she said, though no one was saying a word. "We have a play today and the name of it is — " Before she could finish, Hannie tiptoed over to Karen and whispered a question in her ear. "No, no." Karen said firmly. "You come on *after*."

Karen turned back to the audience. "Like I was saying," she continued, "the name of our play today is *Getting to Be Stars*. I will be the biggest star, and Hannie and Amanda are two other stars. Okay," she said. I think she wasn't sure how to make the transition from her opening speech to the actual play. She walked to the back of the stage, turned around, and walked back again. "Now it's the play," she said simply.

Suddenly, Karen struck a melodramatic pose, her hand across her forehead.

"Oh, dear," she wailed in a high, false voice. "I want to be a star. In fact, I know I'm a star. But the question is, how do I get on TV?"

There was a long pause. Something was obviously supposed to happen, but someone was missing her cue.

"Hannie!" Karen prompted loudly.

"Oh!" Hannie started. She tottered over in her too-big dress-up shoes to deliver her (late) line.

"Did you think of calling up that Darrel boy?" Hannie asked loudly.

"Derek," hissed Karen. "Derek."

"Oh, yeah." Hannie tried again. "Did you think of calling that Derek boy? Maybe he could get you on TV."

"Kristy says no," wailed Karen. She looked directly at Kristy, to make sure the line was having some effect. Then she broke into loud, fake sobs and cried into her arm. She was an actress, all right.

"So what are you going to do?" cried Amanda.

"I'll do the only thing I *can* do," said Karen. Now she was holding her arms grandly up to the sky. "I'll go to Hollywood and be discovered and I'll get lots of costumes and my own dressing room."

Well, you can imagine the rest of the play. Karen did go to Hollywood. She knocked on door after door, but (sob, sob), she couldn't get a job. After many tries, she started thinking that maybe she should go home — crawl back defeated, with her tail betwen her legs.

"Well," she said dramatically. "I'll just try one more door."

She knocked. Amanda answered.

"Who are you?" asked Karen.

"I'm the director," said Amanda. "We've got a show to do here, but my main actress just got sick. I need someone else to step in and be a star."

"I'm a star!" cried Karen.

"Then you're hired!" said the director.

In the last scene of the play, two reporters (Hannie and Amanda) crowded around Karen to interview her. They held up their microphones (which were really a spatula and a soup spoon) for her to speak into.

"What is the secret of your success?" asked Hannie.

"Well," Karen said, smiling, "all along I

knew I was a star. It would've been very easy if I could've met Derek, but I knew, I just *knew*, I had to get on TV."

Hannie and Amanda dropped their microphones and applauded loudly. Karen took a long, low bow. She was some kind of star, all right. Kristy and the rest of the audience joined in the applause.

Later, when Kristy told me about the play, I felt the knot in my stomach again. Oh, I found myself thinking, if only stardom were as easy as that.

CHAPTER 8

On that Saturday when Kristy and her crowd were "getting to be stars" in the safety of their house, I was out in the big, wide world trying to do the same thing. That's because Saturday was my first *Swan Lake* audition.

I can't tell you how crazy I was that morning. You know how usually, when you wake up, it takes awhile to shake the sleep off? Well, that morning, when I opened my eyes, my heart was already racing and adrenalin was already pumping through my veins. One word was pounding in my head: AUDITION! I hopped out of bed and began my morning's work . . . driving my family nuts.

Mama was in the kitchen making coffee. I joined her and started pacing around.

" 'Morning, Jessi," Mama said. She smiled an amused sort of smile. I could tell that she recognized this nervousness of mine. My whole family is used to it. This is the way I always get before an audition or a performance.

The rest of my family drifted into the kitchen and we all sat down for breakfast. At least, they sat down. I kept jumping up from my place. I had to check on the toast, I had to get another spoon, I had to fill my glass with orange juice, and, of course, I had to change my mind and switch to grapefruit.

I caught Daddy throwing Mama his own little amused smile. When breakfast was done, I jumped up from the table.

"I'll do the dishes," I said.

"I have a better idea," said Daddy. "Why don't you go downstairs to your practice room and do some warming up. To tell you the truth, I'm not sure you could hold a plate steady in those hands of yours this morning. Better for you to grab onto something stable, like the barre."

"Right," I said quickly. "Good idea."

Going down to the basement and working at the barre did calm me down some. At least it gave me something to think about. My feet, for instance. I had to work through all the muscles in my toes and up through my ankles. Then, of course, I had to worry about my legs. I stretched my calves and my hamstrings and did some strengthening work. Finally I was ready to put on my toe shoes and work on my balance.

It was a lot of work. But it did keep me occupied until it was time to get ready to leave.

The sheet of instructions Mme Noelle had given me said that I should bring a picture and résumé to the audition. Mama had typed me a short résumé with information about the ballet schools I had gone to and about the few performances I had been in. We stapled a little snapshot of me on top.

I looked it over. I panicked.

"Mama!" I called frantically. "We forgot to put my telephone number on the résumé!"

"No we didn't, honey." Her voice was soft and soothing. "There it is, right there." She pointed to the top of the page. She was right. There it was.

"But the résumé doesn't say anything about *Coppélia*," I rushed on. *Coppélia* was the last performance I had been in.

Mama pointed down the résumé. There, indeed, was *Coppélia*. Mama had included a whole paragraph about it.

"Oh," I said sheepishly. I decided it was time to fix my hair.

I went into the bathroom, brushed my hair back off my face, and pulled it up tightly with an elastic band. I looked at myself in the mirror. It didn't look right. I pulled the elastic band out and tried it again. No good. I must have done this about ten more times when I looked up in the mirror and noticed Daddy standing behind me, watching the whole thing.

"Having trouble?" he asked.

"I can't get all my hair to stay in the elastic, Daddy," I said sullenly. I think I was sort of pouting.

"Did you try glueing it?" Daddy smiled. Of course, he was just trying to tease me out of my mood, but I wouldn't be comforted. Daddy put his arms around me. That felt a little better.

"So why don't we shave your hair all off?" he asked. "I could go get my razor right now. A little off the sides, off the top . . ."

All of a sudden , the whole thing did seem kind of funny. I guess I had been getting a little carried away. I took a look at my hair in the mirror. To tell the truth, it looked just fine. I gave Daddy a kiss, changed into my leotard, and was ready to hit the road.

The audition itself was bigger, scarier, and even more professional than I had imagined. The girls in my ballet class were right. A lot of New York dancers had shown up to try out. They were all long and lean and wore beautiful practice clothes — shiny leotards that showed off every muscle, matching leg warmers, and gauzy ballet skirts with crisp satin ties.

All these ballerinas had their pictures and résumés in hand. Of course, their pictures weren't little snapshots like mine. They were the same kind of fancy head shots that Derek had. Somehow, being at this audition reminded me of my very first ballet class. I remembered the feeling. Mama hadn't had time to buy me ballet slippers, so I had had to take my first class barefoot. But once the class had started, it hadn't mattered. I got right into concentrating on the work.

I looked around me at the audition. Everyone was stretching out and pounding their toe shoes on the floor to soften them up. These are things that ballerinas always do before they go onstage.

"I know how to do all that," I thought confidently.

So I took a deep breath and joined right in.

The audition itself was actually kind of fun. They broke us up into groups and taught us some combinations of steps, some slow ones in which you had to try to be steady and graceful, and some fast ones in which you traveled across the whole stage. I wasn't sure how I did, but I thought I did okay. After my group

70

took its turn, I waited in the back of the theater and watched the others. There was a tight, clique-y group of ballerinas standing near me. They were watching the other groups, too. And they were making nasty comments about everyone onstage.

"Look at her," one of them said. "She has no balance. And look at her leg. It's just flopping there."

I couldn't help but look at the girl they pointed out. It was true, she lost her balance at one point, and it was also true that her leg wasn't as stretched as it could be. But to tell you the truth, she was a beautiful dancer. I thought she was the best onstage.

I moved away from the gossippers. The thing about ballet is that sometimes you come across girls who are sharks — girls who circle around, watching and waiting for someone else to fail. I guess it's because ballet can be so competitive.

"Jessica Ramsey."

What was that? Someone was calling my name. It was the stage manager. She was reading off a list of names, and the girls whose names were called were gathering at the front of the theater. I joined the group.

"Me?" I asked the stage manager. "Did you call Jessica Ramsey?"

The stage manager nodded.

Now this you won't believe. At least, I couldn't. The names they were calling were the ones that had made it through the first audition, the dancers they wanted to see a second time.

Me, Jessica Ramsey! They had called my name!

"Come back next Saturday. Same time," said the stage manager.

You bet I'd be there!

Daddy was waiting outside for me. I hopped in the car. I was talking a mile a minute.

"Daddy, Daddy, I got a callback! They broke us into groups, and of course there were some gossipy ballerinas there, but Daddy, they called *me* back!"

I don't know if Daddy understood all of what I said, but he did manage to get the gist.

When we got home, I raced to the phone to call Mallory and tell her my news.

"That's great!" she squealed.

But by this time, other, shakier thoughts had started to seep into my head.

"Oh, but Mallory, what if I'm not good enough?" I said. "And this audition business is so *scary*. I'm not sure I can go through it another time."

Mallory is my friend for a good reason. She

said all the right things then. She told me all I could do was try. And she said I shouldn't let my fears stop me from doing what I wanted in life. I knew she was right. I'd just never been this *nervous* about anything before.

After Mal had calmed me down, she also told me something that Nicky said about Derek, something about how he was doing in school.

"What?" I said. "Is it John again?"

Mallory said Nicky told her that Derek had gotten into a fight. "Nicky said Derek threw his food all over a kid in the cafeteria."

"Nicky must've got it wrong," I said. "That's probably what the Superbrat did to *Derek*."

"No," Mallory insisted. "Nicky says Derek was the one who threw the food."

This information did not sound good.

"The Superbrat pushed Derek too far," I said decisively.

Poor Derek. Things did not sound like they were getting better at all.

CHAPTER 9

Tuesday

Little kids. They can be so ~~meen meen~~ meen. But then sometimes they can be realy nise. I just wish they would be nicer to Derich. When I babbysat for him this afternoon he told me some of the reelly meen tricks that this one kid John has played on him. But then when we whent to the playground we met some boys from his class and they all ended up playing together fine. Maybe Derick will make frends after all. I've got my fingirs crosed.

As you can see, I wasn't the only one in the Baby-sitters Club involved in the Derek business. When Claudia took an afternoon job sitting for Derek and Todd, she jumped right into the soup. Is that what the expression is, soup? Maybe I mean stew. Now Claudia's got *me* making mistakes. Well, whatever the mess was, Claudia got involved.

When she reached the Masterses' house, the boys had just gotten home from school. Claudia noticed that Derek looked kind of jittery. He kept chewing on his nails and, when she gave them their snack, Derek shredded his napkin into a hundred little pieces.

"How was school today?" Claudia asked.

Derek started in on another napkin.

Luckily, it happened to be a beautiful, sunny afternoon. It was one of those blue-sky days, the kind that only happens a couple of times a year and when it does, you think, This is heaven. Every day should be like this. It was much too pretty to spend the whole afternoon cooped up inside, so Claudia suggested a trip to the school playground.

"Yeah!" cried Todd. No question what his vote was.

Derek wasn't as enthusiastic. He scuffed his shoes around on the kitchen floor before he agreed, and Claudia noticed that when they got to the playground, Derek's eyes darted around, taking a quick survey of the other kids who were there. Most of the kids at the playground were younger, and Derek seemed to relax a little. He straddled the seat of a swing while Claudia pushed Todd.

"During school, I hate this playground," Derek said sullenly.

"You do? Why?" asked Claudia.

" 'Cause out here, anything can happen. The teachers aren't really in charge and the kids can pretty much do anything they want."

"That's exactly what I always liked about the playground," said Claudia.

"Yeah, but that means they can do anything they want to *me*."

"Oh. Right." Claudia remembered. How could she have even forgotten?

Derek looked around again to make sure he didn't see anybody he knew.

"What do the kids do to you?" Claudia asked.

"Well . . ." Derek sighed. "Like the other day, I was on the monkey bars over there and I was just playing. I was hanging upside down, when this guy John came over and pushed my legs off the bar."

"Really?" Claudia gasped. "That's terrible!"

"I landed right on my head," said Derek. He pushed his hair back to show her where. "Do you see a bump?"

"Not really." Claudia squinted. She parted his hair and combed her fingers over his scalp.

"It must've healed," said Derek.

"Still," said Claudia. "That's horrible."

Derek heaved another big sigh.

"Yeah, and then another time, when I was on my way into the school in the morning, John grabbed my book bag, dumped all my stuff onto the ground, and stole my math homework."

"He stole your homework!" Claudia was aghast. Probably because Claudia isn't the best student in the world and she appreciates how hard it is to do homework in the first place. "Well, what did you do?" she asked.

"What *could* I do?" asked Derek. "When Mr. Rossi asked us to pass in our homework, I didn't have any to turn in. I told him I forgot it at home."

Claudia shook her head. She could relate.

"Did the teacher call your parents?" she asked. That would be Claudia's worst nightmare.

"No," said Derek. "I just had to bring it in the next day."

"Well, do the kids ever let you play with them?" asked Claudia.

"Once," said Derek. "They were playing catch. I asked if I could play, too, and they said yes. John tossed me the ball, and I couldn't believe it. I thought, 'This is great.' But when I caught the ball, something sticky got on my fingers. John had stuck ABC gum all over the ball."

"Ick," Claudia said. "Already-been-chewed."

"Right," Derek answered.

Claudia gave Todd another big push.

"Oh, no!" Derek said suddenly. He turned backwards on the swing and tucked his chin down to hide his face.

"What is it?" asked Claudia.

Derek shushed her.

Claudia looked in the direction Derek had turned from. Four boys on bicycles had just ridden onto the playground. They looked like they were about Derek's age. They circled the monkey bars and reared the fronts of their bikes up as if they were cowboys riding wild horses. They headed for the swing set.

"Oh, *no*," Derek said again.

"From your class?" asked Claudia.

"Yeah."

"Don't worry," she said. "They're not going to bother you while I'm here."

When the boys reached the swing set, they hopped off their bikes. Derek turned back around. He sat up straighter.

"Hi," he said cautiously.

"Hi," the boys replied.

Then nobody said anything. The boys stared at Derek. He stared at the ground. Claudia knew that it's usually best to let kids try to work things out for themselves, but after awhile, when everybody was still standing there not saying anything, she just had to jump in. That's when she got her great idea.

"Would you like to join us?" she asked the boys. "I'm Claudia, the baby-sitter, and this is Todd. We were just about to head back to Derek's house. Do you want to come over?"

Derek stared at Claudia, dumbfounded. Each of the boys looked at another.

"Yeah," one said finally. "Sure."

Claudia smiled. That boy was obviously the ringleader. She figured he was probably the infamous John.

Claudia's idea to invite the boys over was a smart one. She had a hunch that it would be good for them to see where Derek lived. They'd see that he was just a regular kid living in a regular house in Stoneybrook.

On the way to the Masterses' house, the boys walked their bikes alongside Derek. Claudia held Todd's hand and walked a little ways away. She kept her ears open, though. The boys still didn't say much of anything.

One sort of muttered, "This the way?"

Another commented briefly, "Hey, I know somebody on this block."

Well, at least what they did say seemed friendly enough.

When they got to Derek's house, Claudia turned into the front walk.

"This is where you live?" asked one of the boys. His mouth was hanging open like he'd just seen a blue elephant.

"Yeah," said Derek.

"I thought you lived in a Disneyland castle or something," the boy said.

Claudia had to stop herself from laughing out loud.

She let the boys inside. They were all eyes. When she described their reaction to me, it sort of reminded me of the first time *I* went to Derek's house. (I wonder if the boys noticed all the old newspapers and the pile of dirty dishes.) The boys looked around at this regular house in total surprise.

"Wow!" one said. "A house."

Derek invited the kids up to his room to play. Claudia decided it would be best if she stayed out of the way a little while. So she and Todd settled into a chair in the living room with a couple of picture books. That would be good for Todd anyway, she figured. Derek gets so much of the attention so often, Todd could use some cozy one-to-one time.

As she turned the pages of Todd's books, she could hear laughter drifting down from Derek's room. It wasn't mean laughter, either. She could hear that boy laughing, the one she figured was John, and she could hear Derek joining right in. As she sat there, Claudia congratulated herself. She figured she'd solved the Superbrat problem once and for all.

After awhile the boys trooped down the stairs.

"Hey, Derek, that was fun," one said.

"Yeah, I never played that game before," said another.

"I got it in California," said Derek.

"Wow. Cool. See you in school tomorrow, okay?"

The boys had obviously had a good time. They waved a quick good-bye to Claudia and ran outside to their bicycles. Derek stood at the doorway, waving, as his new friends coasted down the driveway and skidded out onto the sidewalk. When he closed the door, he was all smiles.

"Hey," said Claudia, "not bad, huh?"

"Yeah," Derek said. He looked truly amazed. "They liked me. We had fun."

"So which one was John?" Claudia asked. She could hardly wait to get the information.

"John?" Derek looked puzzled. "Oh. John. None of them," he said. "John isn't friends with them."

Derek wandered back up to his room. He looked a little dazed from the events of the afternoon. Dazed, but happy.

Well, Claudia thought, she hadn't exactly solved the Superbrat problem, but she had helped some of the boys to be friends with Derek, and that was a good start.

"See you tomorrow in school," they had said.

Not bad for one afternoon of baby-sitting.

CHAPTER 10

The next Saturday was the day of my second audition. I also had another job scheduled at the Masterses'. Mrs. Masters had offered to pick me up after the audition and bring me straight to their house. You can bet my parents went for that idea in a big way. They end up carting me around so much for my classes that I think they sometimes feel like a ballet chauffeur service.

I told Mrs. Masters where the theater was and what time to come, and sure enough, when I came down from the stage after my audition, I spotted her and Derek standing at the back of the theater. I waved to them and they waved back.

"Jessica Ramsey."

It was the stage manager again, calling my name from the front row of seats. She was sitting next to the choreographer, who was leaning over her, writing something on her pad. For a moment, I felt pretty scared.

It was time to take myself in hand and give myself another little talk.

Come on, I said to myself. They're not going to wait all day while you stand here trying to find your legs.

"Yes?" I asked when I reached them. My voice cracked as the word came out.

"Miss Ramsey," said the stage manager. "Congratulations. You've survived another round. We'd like to see you again next Saturday for the final audition."

"Really?" I squeaked. "I mean, thank you. I mean, I'll see you next week. Thank you very much."

I backed away, all smiles. Then I grabbed my bag, slipped my pants on over my tights, and ran to the back of the theater, where Derek and his mother were waiting.

"You made the cut?" Derek asked. "They asked you back?" I guess he could tell by the big smile that had taken over my face.

"Yup," I said. "Just one more audition to go."

Mrs. Masters gave me a hug of congratulations and Derek slapped me five. As we walked out of the theater to the car, Derek nudged me and pointed to the clique-y group of girls who were again standing at the back of the theater, huddled and whispering.

"Those girls are cutthroat, huh?" Derek said.

"We were standing next to them for awhile," Mrs. Masters added. "They didn't have a nice word to say about anyone."

I shrugged.

"They're a certain type you find around ballet," I said. "But most ballerinas aren't like that."

When we got to the car, Derek pulled a small notepad out of his pocket.

"I took a few notes on your performance," he said.

"You did?" I asked, surprised.

"I hope you don't mind. It really was super. Even I could tell that. But there were a few things that you could just clean up, and since you do have one last audition to go through, I figured I might as well give you some tips."

"Sure," I said. "Shoot." Though, to tell the truth, I was wondering what kind of corrections Derek could really give me about ballet. It's a pretty exacting art, and you sort of have to know a lot about it to be able to notice what's right and what's wrong.

Derek opened his notepad.

"Well," he said. "To start, during the *piqué* turns, you weren't attaching your foot to the back of your knee."

I stared at Derek dumbfounded. How did he know about *piqué* turns? How did *he* know where your foot was supposed to be?

"And another note," said Derek. "During the *tour jetés* your spot wandered."

Tour jetés? Spot? Where was Derek getting this technical language? These were the kinds of things Mme Noelle was always hounding me about.

I looked at Derek. He was grinning. I grabbed the notebook out of his hands.

"Give me that," I said.

I looked over the page. It was filled with lots more notes that were just as technical. The only thing he had wrong was the spelling of the words. For instance, he had spelled *"tour jeté"* the way it is pronounced — "toor jetay."

"All right," I said. "How did you come up with these notes?"

"Certain cutthroat types can be very helpful without knowing it."

"You mean . . . ?"

"We were standing by those girls for an awfully long time," Mrs. Masters explained. "We heard them tearing apart everyone's performance, so Derek got the idea to see what they had to say about yours. They have trained eyes and were very specific in what they saw. Derek just happened to get it all down on paper."

I looked over the notes. They were actually very helpful. I recognized a lot of the mistakes they had caught. They were things I often did wrong. Well, now I had the whole week to work on them.

"Gee, I don't know who I should thank," I said. "You or the cutthroats."

"You can thank me," Derek grinned. "I accept all donations of money, all presents, all major credit cards . . ."

I cuffed Derek playfully on the head.

"All bops on the head," he continued, "all punches on the arm . . ."

"All punches in the *nose*," I said, laughing.

"All kicks in the shins."

I have to admit, we were getting pretty silly. Suddenly, I remembered that I was supposed to be the baby-sitter. I glanced at Mrs. Masters to see if she seemed bothered. Mrs. Masters smiled.

"All knocks to the noggin," she joined in.

Pretty soon we were all laughing. For me it was a way of letting out some of that giddiness that was left over from the audition.

"You know, those notes are all fine and

good," Mrs. Masters said, "but we did catch your performance and I just want to say that it was beautiful."

"Really?" I said.

"Breathtaking," she went on. "There's just something about ballet, isn't there? And you looked like such a natural ballerina up on that stage."

"Except for the *piqué* turns and the *tour jetés*," Derek teased.

"I think those girls were picking on you because you were so good," said Mrs. Masters.

Boy, I sure wished I could let myself believe that. I still wasn't sure I had the stuff to make it into the production. Now that I had only one more audition to go, I started to get *really* scared. I was in the big league now. Deep down, I was afraid of blowing it.

By this time Mrs. Masters was pulling the car into the driveway. When she shut off the ignition, she turned to face Derek.

"Well," she said, "are you going to tell Jessi your news?"

Derek blushed.

"Shhh," he said.

"News?" My ears pricked up. "What news?"

"I'll tell you later," Derek said.

The front door of the house banged open. Todd had heard the car and was running out to greet us. He jumped right into my arms.

"Jessi!" he cried.

I set him down and followed him into the house. Mr. Masters was putting on his jacket to join his wife, who was waiting for him in the car. A few moments later, I was alone with the kids. My curiosity was getting stronger and stronger.

"So," I said. "What's this news all about, anyway?"

"Nothing." Derek shrugged.

Todd grabbed my arm and started jumping up and down.

"We're going back to L.A.! We're going back to L.A.!" he said.

"What!?" I shrieked.

Derek stared at the floor.

"Derek, are you really?" I asked.

He glanced up quickly, then nodded his head.

"Why?" I asked. "You just got here."

"Derek's gonna be on TV again," Todd said. "He's gonna be on another show."

"A TV movie," Derek explained. "They start shooting real soon, so we have to leave in a couple of weeks."

"A couple of weeks?" I said. I couldn't believe it. This had all happened so fast.

"I'm gonna go back to my old school," said Todd. He was still hanging on my arm and tugging hard.

"Just when I started to make friends," said Derek. "I'll miss my new friends and I'll miss you. . . . Oh, no, Jessi," he cried. "I just realized. I won't get to see you in *Swan Lake*." Derek's eyes started to glaze over. You could tell his mind was wandering off somewhere. "Hey," he said suddenly. "Jessi, why don't you come out to L.A., too? There're lots of dancers out there. You could pick up some modeling work. I'm sure you could get some commercials."

"I can't go out to L.A.," I protested.

"Why not?" said Derek. "I did."

"Anyway, I couldn't get work on commercials."

"Sure you could." Derek grabbed my free hand and started tugging at me, too.

"Come to L.A.," he started chanting. "Come to L.A."

Todd joined in.

With Derek tugging on one hand and Todd tugging on the other, I felt a little bit like a giant piece of taffy. Just then, the doorbell rang.

"Saved by the bell!" I said with a laugh.

Todd ran to the window to see who was there.

"It's your friends," he called to Derek.

Derek looked at me quickly.

"Don't say anything about L.A.," he said. "I'll tell them. Soon, but not yet."

He ran to the door. Four boys trooped in. I guess they were the same boys Claudia had invited over. Derek introduced me to them, but none of them was named John.

Oh, well. I sighed to myself. Derek had been in Stoneybrook such a short time. It had been long enough for him to make a few friends, but not long enough to win over the Superbrat. I took Todd's hand and brought him out to play in the backyard. There sure were big changes here. And something Derek had said was echoing in my brain. That *I* could get modeling jobs and work on commercials.

"Come on, Todd," I said.

Modeling. Commercials. That might be a relief after all this ballet anxiety. I had a lot to think about.

CHAPTER 11

When Monday rolled around, I almost missed the meeting of the Baby-sitters Club. I had two projects in mind, and both of them had something to do with Derek. At 5:10, I was still sitting in my room, working on Project #1. I had the Stamford phone book in my lap. I opened it to the yellow pages and was copying down names and phone numbers of certain kinds of businesses. I had closed the door because I didn't want anyone to know what I was doing . . . at least not yet. It was my secret. I bet I have you curious about what I was up to. Well, I'll give you this hint: the project had something to do with Derek's idea about me going into acting and modeling. I hadn't been able to stop thinking about the possibility, ever since Derek had brought it up.

I glanced at the clock. Uh-oh! Only a few minutes to meeting time. Time to put aside Project #1 and get started on Project #2.

(You'll see what *that* one was in a minute.) I hid the list of phone numbers under my pillow and took off for Claudia's.

No one was surprised, of course, when I slid into the meeting at the very last minute. I guess at this point, they almost expect that. Kristy was already rapping on the arm of her director's chair to call the club members to attention.

"The Baby-sitters Club will now come to order," she said.

I sat up as tall as I could. I don't usually talk a lot at the meetings, being a junior officer and all, but like I said, I had to start organizing this second project I had in mind. And that would mean getting all the club members involved.

"Anybody have any club business?" Kristy asked.

I shot up my hand even though Kristy had said at my first club meeting that I didn't have to do that.

Kristy looked a little surprised and so did everyone else. I hadn't even told Mallory my idea yet.

"Jessi," Kristy called on me.

"Yes. Well," I began. "Well, all of you know by now that Derek and his family are moving back to L.A. in a couple of weeks. So my idea is . . . My idea is . . ." I swallowed hard. "My idea is that we give him a surprise good-bye party before he leaves. We could invite all the new friends he's made. That way everybody will get a chance to say good-bye."

For a moment nobody said anything. Then Kristy's face broke into a big smile.

"Great idea!" she said.

"Yeah!" Mallory echoed.

"I could make invitations," said Claudia.

Everybody started talking at once.

"We could invite some of the kids we baby-sit for."

"And all the kids in Derek's class."

"*All* the kids?" I asked. That sounded like a big crowd. "I was thinking of having the party at my house. I don't know if everyone would fit."

"Well, we could have it at my house," Kristy offered. Kristy's house, remember, is a mansion.

"Really?" I said. "You wouldn't mind?"

"It would sure make Karen happy," Kristy said, laughing. "She still hasn't given up the idea of meeting Derek and asking him to make her a star."

A phone call came in and then another one, so we did have to do some of our usual meeting stuff, but we spent most of the time planning the party. Kristy, who loves to be in charge, had quickly taken over.

The first problem we ran into was the question of when to hold the party. There wasn't much time left before Derek would be moving again and we were all pretty tightly scheduled with jobs and all. Mary Anne paged through the appointment pages of the record book.

"Hmm," she said. "Looks like the only time might be Saturday afternoon."

"No, we can't do it then," said Dawn. "Remember, I just took that job at the Newtons'."

That was the last call that had come in. In all the excitement, Mary Anne had forgotten to write it down.

"Anyway, Saturday afternoon's no good because that's when Jessi has her final *Swan Lake* audition," Mallory piped up.

Oh, no. I shot Mallory a withering glance. Why did she have to tell the whole club about that?

"You do?" Mary Anne asked, all excited. "You mean you got through the other auditions? Why didn't you tell us?"

Suddenly, everyone surrounded me, giving me their congratulations and asking me questions. I didn't know why, but I felt very uncomfortable. This was a new feeling that had taken over. After Saturday and the initial rush of making the cut, I didn't want to talk about *Swan Lake*. I didn't even want to think about it. All I wanted was to get the last audition over with.

Lucky thing the phone rang then. Another job call came in. Everyone settled back into their places and left me alone.

Mallory was watching me. She could see I looked kind of squirmy.

"Why didn't you want everyone to know?" she whispered.

"I don't know." I shrugged.

After the phone call, Kristy rapped again on the arm of her chair.

"So when are we going to have this party?" she said. "It looks like the only time available would be some night at midnight."

Mary Anne looked over the pages of the appointment book.

"That's not the only time," she said thoughtfully. "If we can't have it Saturday afternoon, how about Saturday morning? Hey, I have an idea! It could be a breakfast party. We could have it from nine until twelve."

"Great idea," cried Kristy. "We could have a table with a whole assortment of cereals."

"And juices," said Dawn.

"A *breakfast* party?" said Claudia. She didn't sound at all sure about the idea.

"Yeah," said Mallory. "A breakfast party. "It's so unusual. It's a great idea."

"But if it's breakfast, we can't serve cake," said Claudia. "Or ice cream. Or cookies. Well," she said with a sigh. You could see the wheels turning in her head. "I guess we could have doughnuts."

All the rest of us laughed.

"Doughnuts, cereal, and juice." Mary Anne wrote all the suggestions down.

"And fruit slices," Dawn added.

Claudia crinkled her nose.

We decided that we would each be responsible for bringing two boxes of cereal, and we divided up the rest of the food equally. (Guess who got doughnuts.) Kristy put Mallory in charge of getting the names of all of Derek's classmates, since her brother Nicky was in the same class. That brought up one last issue for discussion.

"Are you going to invite John?" Mallory asked.

"John?" Kristy looked puzzled.

"The Superbrat," Claudia explained.

Everyone looked to me for the answer.

"I think we should invite him," I said. "If we're inviting the whole class, we have to. Anyway, this may be Derek's last chance to win the kid over."

"And I want to *meet* John finally," said Claudia. "I'm dying to know who the Superbrat is."

That settled that.

When the meeting broke up, I headed home for dinner. Becca was already setting the table, but I slipped upstairs to my room and fished out the phone list from under my pillow. Time to get back to Project #1. I went back down to the kitchen, helped Mama put the food onto plates, and waited until everyone was seated and Daddy was helping himself to butter for his mashed potatoes.

I cleared my throat.

"Mama, Daddy?" I said.

"Yes?" Daddy answered.

I had rehearsed a whole speech, thinking of just the way I wanted to present my idea, but suddenly I couldn't remember what I had planned to say.

"I was talking to Derek," I said.

Becca dropped her fork. I think she figured she was about to get more information about Lamont. Sorry, Becca, no such luck.

"Well," I stumbled on, "Derek suggested that I move out to L.A."

"Move to L.A.?" Now it was Mama's turn to drop her fork.

"I mean, I don't want to go to L.A.," I said quickly. "But Derek suggested I come to L.A. so I could do some modeling or get on commercials. Anyway, that made me think. I might be able to do that here, the way Derek did before he got on TV. There are some modeling and talent agencies in Stamford, and I think they do local commercials and some newspaper and magazine ads."

I pulled out the list of numbers I had taken down and passed it to Mama.

"I was thinking of calling them," I said, "to see if they might be interested in me, but, of course, I wanted to check with you first."

Mama looked at Daddy. He was already looking at her. Squirt smashed his spoon into his mashed potatoes.

"Po-po!" he cried.

Mama handed the list over to Daddy and he looked it over, too. For the longest time, I thought no one was going to say anything.

"Why do you think you want to do this?" Daddy asked.

I wasn't prepared for that question.

"I don't know," I said. "I just do."

"You've got quite a full schedule already with ballet class and the Baby-sitters Club," Mama said.

"And who knows, you may have a full *Swan Lake* rehearsal schedule coming up," Daddy added.

"I'm probably not going to get into that," I mumbled.

Daddy shot a look at Mama. "Are you nervous about *Swan Lake*?" he asked.

"I'm not nervous," I said. "I just don't *care* anymore."

"Mmm-hmm," Daddy said. He didn't sound like he believed me.

"Well," I said, "maybe I do care, but I'll tell you, this audition process is driving me crazy. And after I go through all this, I'm probably not going to make it anyway. So it seems to me that I might as well branch out, get some other kinds of work. Modeling can't be as nerve-racking as ballet. I mean, all you have to do is stand there and smile, right?"

Mama wiped mashed potatoes off of Squirt's cheeks and chin.

"Well, if you want to look into this," she said, "I don't see why you shouldn't. Why don't you go ahead and make some phone calls. You can find out some more information, and then we'll talk again."

"As long as it's limited to Stamford," Daddy added.

"Right," Mama agreed. "That's as far as this chauffeur service goes."

"Really?" I jumped up from the table. "I can call?"

"Well, not right now," said Daddy, laughing. "I think agencies are closed this time of night, and besides, you've got a plateful of dinner to eat."

"Oh. Right," I said.

I sat back down at the table and poked at the food on my plate. Becca was still staring at me. Her mouth was gaping and she hadn't yet picked up her fork.

"You mean you're going to be a TV star, too?" she said.

"Tee-vee!" Squirt cried.

Daddy, Mama, and I just laughed.

CHAPTER 12

By midweek, party plans were in full swing. I had made a couple of secret calls to Mrs. Masters to clear the date with her and make sure that she could get Derek and Todd to the party on time. Of course, Mr. and Mrs. Masters thought that the party was a great idea.

"We're very touched that you girls have spent so much time helping Derek readjust," she said. "I don't know how he would have done it without you."

I was practically beaming on the other end of the phone. It's true, I thought. The Babysitters Club is special that way.

That Wednesday I was scheduled for another sitting job at the Masterses'. Before Mrs. Masters left to go out that day, she wanted to offer some last-minute help with the party. Of course, that was not the easiest thing to do with Derek standing right there, but she managed to get the information across anyway.

It was a funny exchange. First she winked at me. "Tell your mother I have those bowls she wanted," she said. She emphasized the word "bowls" as if it had great significance.

"Bowls?" I asked blankly. I didn't get what she was talking about.

Mrs. Masters winked again, this time more obviously.

"You know what I'm talking about. Those disposable *picnic* bowls and those plastic spoons?" she said. "Your mother had called me up and asked me where to get them. Well, I happened to go to the store myself and bought plenty. More than enough. So tell your mother I'll give them to her."

"Oh," I caught on. *"Bowls."*

Derek gave us an odd look. I guess it was obvious something was going on.

"And do you think your mother would like, maybe, some bagels and cream cheese?" Mrs. Masters asked. "I could bring over some of those, too."

"Bagels and cream cheese?" I considered that. "I think my mother would *love* bagels and cream cheese. That's a great idea. She could have them Saturday *morning* with her *breakfast*."

"And does she need milk?" asked Mrs. Masters.

Derek looked from his mother to me.

"Is your mother sick or something?" he asked.

"Who? My mother?" I said guiltily. "No, she's fine. Why?"

"Oh," Derek looked puzzled. "It just sounds like she can't get to the store by herself or something."

"Oh, you know how mothers are," Mrs. Masters said airily. "Sometimes they like to have milk with their bagels."

It wasn't quite an answer and it didn't make much sense, but Mrs. Masters gave me a last wink and breezed out the door.

"You two sound cuckoo," said Derek.

"Cuckoo," Todd echoed. "Let's play cuckoo bird."

Since neither Derek nor I knew any game called "cuckoo bird," and the truth was Todd probably didn't, either, we decided to play Chinese checkers instead.

While we were setting up the board, Derek asked me about *Swan Lake.*

"Are you excited about the last audition?" he asked.

"Not really," I answered. "I'm not thinking about it much."

"Why not?" asked Derek.

"I'm just not," I said. I wanted to change

the subject. "But I *am* thinking about starting modeling like you suggested. And I do want to ask you some questions about how you got started here in Stamford."

"Okay," Derek said.

I had plenty of questions and Derek had plenty of answers. He told me the names of some people I might call and what to expect if I went in to talk with them.

"The agents'll take you through it step by step," he said. "They'll tell you what kind of work you'd be good for, and they'll even set you up with a photographer if you want."

"A photographer?" I asked.

"For head shots and things like that."

"Is that expensive?"

"Yeah, but you make the money back on your first job."

"Right," I said. This was sounding a little complicated, but Derek didn't think so. He was just getting started.

"First they'll probably get you newspaper work and then magazines and then commercials. And then you'll probably land a TV series, just like me."

"Right." I laughed.

"That'll be great!" Derek was serious. "Then you'll *have* to move out to L.A. You could stay at my house as long as you want. I'm sure

Mom won't care. You could be sort of like a sister."

"Then you could baby-sit for us all the time!" Todd cried out.

"She might not have time to baby-sit," Derek said seriously. "Once she's got the TV series, she'll be taping all day."

Todd's face fell.

"Couldn't you baby-sit just sometimes?" he asked.

I gave him a hug.

"Sure," I said. "But don't count on my coming out to L.A. any time soon. Maybe when I'm older and out of school or something. Right now I think I'll just try to get some work in Stamford."

Derek jumped one of his Chinese-checker marbles over three of mine.

"Gotcha!" he said.

I guess I hadn't been paying much attention to the game. My head had been spinning with all these new show biz plans. Forget ballet, I was thinking. Being famous and on a TV series was starting to sound like a lot more fun.

I stretched my legs out on either side of me on the floor.

"Oh, yeah. Don't forget to tell these agents that you're a ballerina," Derek reminded me. "That's a real plus."

"A ballerina," I said vaguely. "Yeah."

After the sitting job (Derek creamed me three times at Chinese checkers and even Todd beat me once), I did my usual sprint over to Claudia's house for the Wednesday meeting, which again turned into more of a planning session for the party.

Claudia had the invitations she had made spread out all over the floor. Everybody was crowded around them, ooh-ing and ah-ing. The invitations were very clever. Claudia had cut the cards into the shape of TV sets and she had drawn a picture of a cereal commercial on the screens.

"Start your day the party way," she had written on the inside. And then she listed all the necessary information. Since there was still work to be done on the invitations, Mary Anne and Dawn helped Claudia write out the insides, and Kristy and Mallory got busy copying onto envelopes names and addresses from the class list Mallory had brought.

I looked over Mallory's shoulder and scanned down the list of names. "Ricky, Betsy, Amy, Tommy," it read. I looked down the names again. There was no one named John.

"Hey," I said, picking up the list. "How come the Superbrat isn't on here?"

"Oh, yeah," said Mallory. "I tried to call

you. When I asked Nicky about John, he looked completely confused. He said there's no kid by that name in the class."

"No John?" I said. "There's gotta be."

"I told him it was the kid who was the Superbrat. I mean, I didn't use that word, but I said the kid who was really bothering Derek."

"Well, what'd Nicky say?"

"He didn't know what I was talking about. He said all the boys had been bothering Derek for awhile, but that had pretty much stopped and that Derek has a lot of friends now."

"Hmm," I said. I tried to think back on what Derek had told me. "Maybe he never actually said that John was in his class. Maybe John is from a different class or even from an older grade."

"That could be it," said Mallory.

Since my friends had grabbed up all the invitations and there was nothing much for me to do, I stationed myself by the phone and took calls. In between calls, I placed my leg up on Claudia's bed to stretch it out. Without knowing I was doing it, I started humming the music from *Swan Lake*.

Mallory looked over and smiled.

"Practicing to be a swan?" she asked.

"Hmm?" She jolted me away from my thoughts. "Me? No," I said. "Actually, I was thinking of some calls I have to make. Derek gave me a lot of new tips."

Around me, my friends worked away on the invitations, and though I half listened to their conversation, I wasn't fully in the room. In my mind, I was somewhere in Stamford, in a fancy agent's office. A box of glossy head shots was at my side and the agent was handing me a contract.

"I'll make you a star, kid," he was saying. He lit a cigar and slapped me on the back. "You've got the face. We'll plaster your picture in every magazine across the country."

My face. In every magazine across the country. I heaved a big sigh. I probably wouldn't even have *time* to be in *Swan Lake*.

CHAPTER 13

Party day! Saturday arrived quickly. Well, "quickly" might be putting it mildly. Actually, it arrived like a runaway train. There were lots of last-minute plans to get straight, and everybody in the club was calling everybody else.

Mallory called Kristy about the guest list.

"Nicky says that most of the kids are going to be able to come. Do you think we need another few cartons of juice?"

Kristy called Mary Anne about the benches.

"We'll push the picnic tables together and borrow some more from the neighbors, but we're short five chairs. Can you bring some of those folding ones?"

Even as late as Saturday morning, the phone calls were still going strong. On her way to the party, Claudia called Kristy from the doughnut shop.

"Do you think kids like chocolate doughnuts

better than coconut?" she asked.

"Who cares, Claudia?" Kristy snapped. I guess Kristy had plenty to think about already. "Get them all. Get an assortment!"

For my part, I had set my alarm for very early that morning. The day was going to be a big one for me. I not only had the party in the morning, I had my final audition (yipes!) right after. I slipped down to my barre in the basement to wake up my sleepy and very tight muscles. Mmmmm. It always feels so good to get stretched out.

That morning I would've liked to have had a long time at the barre, but I did have to get to the party early, and that left time pretty scrunched up. Mama had promised to pick me up after the party and get me to the audition early so I could do a real warm-up there. (Thank you, Mama.) That morning I had just enough time to throw my toe shoes, leg warmers, and leotard into my dance bag and gather up all the party supplies I had promised to bring. I called Becca (of course, she was invited to the party, too) and hoisted my bags into my arms. Mr. Spier pulled into the driveway with Mary Anne to give us a ride to the party. I hurried out to the car and dropped my bags onto the backseat.

"Did you remember to bring your — ?"

Mary Anne didn't even have to finish the sentence.

"Oh, no!" I cried. "Just a minute, okay?"

I raced back into the house, up to my room, and grabbed my bathrobe off its hook.

That's right. My bathrobe. This was a goofy idea Kristy had had, and it seemed so silly, we all thought it was great. Her idea was that since it was a *breakfast* party, all the members of the club should wear bathrobes over their clothes. Since we'd be keeping our eye on so many kids, and since we didn't know a lot of them to begin with, the bathrobes would be kind of like a uniform, and the kids would at least know who was in charge. Kristy had wanted us to go even further with the joke and have us all wear curlers in our hair, too, but Mary Anne and Claudia vetoed that idea right away. I think neither of them wanted to be seen in curlers in public, and the truth was, neither did I.

"Bathrobes are funny enough," Claudia had said.

"How about if we just wear curler caps, then?" Kristy had suggested.

Maybe the party plans had started to get to her.

"Kristy," Claudia said firmly, "this is a good-bye party, not a *Halloween* party."

"Right," Kristy had said.

By the time Mary Anne, Becca, and I arrived at Kristy's house that morning, all the other club members were there. They were throwing paper tablecloths over the picnic tables and setting the places with plates, bowls, and cups.

Mallory was busy farther back in the yard, setting up the one game we had planned. To fit in with the "Good Morning" theme, we had come up with a funny idea for a relay race. The teams of kids would line up and, to start the race, we were going to set off an alarm clock. Each runner had to put on a pair of pants, drink a cup of imaginary juice (we thought it might be dangerous to use real juice since someone might choke), run a comb through his or her hair, grab a book bag, and run to pass the book bag to a teammate across the yard.

Not to sound conceited, but the whole idea for the relay was mine. That's exactly how I feel every morning, like getting ready for school is a relay race. But I can't take all the credit. Mallory was the one who had the idea for the prizes. She had spent the whole morning fishing those little prize packages out of all our cereal boxes. Every kid on the winning team would get one.

Soon the kids began arriving. Of course, we had told them to get there ahead of time so that when Derek arrived, everyone would be gathered for the surprise. The yard started filling up. We club members scattered ourselves around to talk to the kids and keep some kind of general order. The back door opened and Kristy's sister Karen came out to join us. Oh no. She was wearing her "Getting to Be Stars" costume — high heels, gloves, hat, and all. Kristy rolled her eyes good-naturedly.

"You're going to wear that for the relay race?" she asked.

"I have to wear it so Derek'll notice me," Karen answered. "It shows I'm a star."

She started across the yard to the picnic tables, her heels sinking into the sod with each step.

I'll tell you, maybe Claudia was wrong. Between Karen in her getup and all of us baby-sitters in our bathrobes, that party might as well have been for Halloween.

Inside, the kitchen phone rang. Kristy's mom answered it and came to the door to call me.

"Jessi," she said, "it's Mrs. Masters."

114

Everyone in the yard let out a little gasp. We were all getting excited. The surprise is always the most fun part.

Mrs. Masters was ready to bring Derek and Todd over and was calling to warn us. She and her husband had told the boys that they were going shopping to buy clothes before the move back to California.

"Coast clear?" Mrs. Masters asked.

"Bring them over," I said. "We're ready and waiting."

The time between the phone call and their arrival seemed like ten years. The kids started to get really giddy. To tell the truth, so did I. Finally, we heard a car pull into the front drive. Everyone started shushing everyone else. The back door opened again. I heard Mrs. Masters talking to Kristy's mom. Then Mrs. Masters called Derek and Todd.

"Come on, boys," she said. "I promise, we'll head out for the mall in a minute. But before we go I just want to show you something."

Derek stepped out of the house and into the yard.

"Surprise!" we all yelled.

He stood there, frozen to the spot. But he didn't have time to be shocked for long, because in a few seconds we were all crowded around him, laughing and talking.

"Were you surprised?"

"Your whole class is here."

"Did you suspect anything?"

"Okay, let's break out the cereal!"

That last cry was from Kristy. She rounded up all the kids and herded them to the tables. The rest of us busied ourselves passing around food.

The kid next to me put three doughnuts on his plate and nothing else — no bagels, no Cheerios, and certainly no fruit slices.

"Hey, Claudia!" I yelled across the tables. "You've got a friend over here!"

We were all laughing and joking and having a good time.

Derek was sitting at the table with me. Across from him were his mom, his dad, and Todd, and next to him were Nicky and some of the other boys. It was great for me to watch him just sitting and talking like a regular kid with his new friends. It was a happy ending, all right. Or, who knows, maybe some kind of beginning, too. I was still curious about John and what had happened with that, but I knew I'd have to wait until sometime when Derek and I were alone to ask him about it. It was clear I wasn't going to get him alone at this party.

116

After the kids finished eating, we let them hang out for awhile before we started the relay race. (We didn't want breakfast to come back up all over the lawn.)

When it was time for the race, Karen had still not changed out of her "star" outfit, and she was hanging around Derek like a fly around honey. The funny thing was, after all her scheming, she was too afraid to open her mouth and actually say anything to him. Finally, Kristy took Karen's hand.

"Derek, did you meet my sister?" Kristy asked. "This is Karen. She's really been wanting to meet you."

Derek had a funny look on his face, like he didn't quite know what to make of Karen's outfit. Karen pulled up her gloves and steadied her hat.

"Hi," she said.

Suddenly, Becca was right behind her.

"Derek!" Becca broke in. "Since you're going back to L.P., do you think you could get me Lamont's autograph?"

Well, okay. So, even as he was leaving, Derek still had to deal with two stage-struck little girls. But two kids out of a whole yardful didn't seem so bad.

"Hey, Derek!" cried one of his classmates. "Come on! Join our team!"

By this time Claudia had organized all the kids into groups for the relay. They were lined up and ready to run.

"On your mark . . . get set . . . wake up!" she cried as the alarm clock sounded.

It was funny to watch the kids struggle with the pants and cheer each other on. All in all, it was a great party. Though Derek would be leaving in a week, we were sending him off with a very nice good-bye.

"Jessi." I spun around. Mama had arrived to pick me up and take me to the audition.

"Is it already time?" I asked.

"Now or never," she said with a smile.

Becca and I called good-bye and followed Mom to the car.

"Break a leg, Jess!" Derek yelled after me. That's show biz talk. What he really meant was "good luck."

So. One event down and one to go.

The final audition. I took a deep breath.

Well, I thought to myself, this is it.

CHAPTER 14

When we reached the theater, I changed into my dance clothes, found myself a quiet corner, and began the extensive warm-up I had planned. The warm-up really helped to calm me down. My head was still full of partying and relay races. I had to shift to ballet.

As I was stretching, I looked around me. Actually the place didn't seem quite so scary anymore. The stage manager and choreographer were talking in the front seats, and the piano accompanist was also warming up, playing scales and snatches of *Swan Lake* themes. I didn't see any of the clique-y "gossip girls" — I guess they'd all been cut — but all around me other ballerinas were going up to their toes, testing their balance. Those of us who were left had all staked out little bits of territory for ourselves. In a funny way, the place was almost beginning to feel like home.

Suddenly, I could really imagine coming

here and performing. It'd be like this every night, I thought, and that'd be great. There is something magical about all the backstage goings-on in a theater — all the performers getting ready and then going out, transformed, before an audience. For a moment I let a picture of myself onstage slip into my thoughts. I was one of the swan maidens and I was costumed in a beautiful white, feathery tutu. It made me so happy just to *think* of myself up there.

Well, I thought quickly, I'll know when I leave today whether or not I got into the production. And if I don't make it, I'll just pursue modeling. That would keep me busy. It'd be something new and different. And it couldn't possibly be as difficult — or as nerve-racking — as ballet.

The stage manager clapped her hands to call together all us ballerinas.

"We look like a flock of migrating birds," I heard one joke.

"Swans," another one answered. "We want to be *swans*."

I closed my eyes for a moment. Suddenly, Mme Noelle's words ran through my head. "You're a gifted dancer," she'd said. Well, we would see. I took a deep breath.

The choreographer taught us a long, difficult

dance variation, but this time, it was pretty easy to pick up. It was really not much different from the ones we'd learned before. Then he divided us into groups. Oh, no. I was in the first one. That meant I wouldn't even get to watch another group and have time to run the variation through my head. Oh, well, I thought. It'll just be like plunging into a pool.

Actually, I think I danced very well. The choreographer had stuck me front row center onstage, which usually makes me nervous. But this time the music was really in my body. When I lifted my arms up, I could feel my whole torso stretch with them. When I extended a leg, I let it suspend there for a moment before I snapped it down. This is exactly what I love about ballet. Once you've got the technique, you can really express yourself.

In the last couple of steps, I did make a small goof. I rushed a step and then had to slow down to get back on count. I didn't know if the choreographer caught it, or if he did, how much it would count against me. Well, I'm human, I thought. What could I do?

After my group had finished, I found a seat in the audience to watch the others. No doubt about it, the competition was stiff. There were some ballerinas I liked better than others, but, the truth was, we were all good. I couldn't

121

imagine how they would choose among us.

Finally, the last group finished and the girls trickled offstage. I wandered up to stand by the stage manager and wait for the news. The stage manager and choreographer had their heads together, bent over their notes. The stage manager glanced up quickly.

"Okay, everybody," she called. "Thank you very much. We'll talk to you in a few days."

A few days? What did she mean? All the other ballerinas had picked up their things and were drifting out the door.

"Excuse me," I said. "Did you say a few days?"

"That's right," she smiled. "You can call the office on Wednesday."

"You mean we're not going to find out today? I have to wait until Wednesday?"

"Yes. That information was on the audition notice," she told me.

Now, how had I missed that?

"Don't worry," she said. I guess I looked pretty upset. "Wednesday will be here before you know it."

"Well, thanks," I managed to reply as I started walking toward the door.

"By the way," the stage manager called after me. "Nice audition."

"Thanks," I called back, this time a little brighter.

But till Wednesday? I had to wait until Wednesday?

Right after I got home that day, the phone rang. It was Mallory, wanting to know if I'd made it or not.

"I don't know," I wailed. "I have to wait four more days!"

"That doesn't seem fair," Mallory said.

"Mallory," I said patiently, "nothing's fair in love or ballet."

On Monday, Mallory came home from school with me to keep me company. Poor Mallory. I think I was pretty jittery. I'd told her a little bit about my modeling plans, and I asked her if she minded if I made a few phone calls. Mallory nodded half-heartedly. She stretched out on our couch and began her homework. I got out the index cards I had started. On the top of each card I had written an agent's name and phone number. When I called and got through, I wrote the information he or she gave me onto the card. Information like, "Head shot necessary" or "Print work only."

That afternoon I was on the phone for at least fifteen minutes with one agent. I could see Mallory peek up from her books every now and again to watch me. While I was still on that call, Daddy got home from work. He was early. It wasn't even time to leave for our club meeting. He dropped his briefcase on a chair, listened in on my conversation, and smiled at Mallory. Mallory had started to look a little nervous. Probably because I sounded so businesslike, and that's not the usual me.

"Hi, you two," Daddy said when I hung up. Then, "How's the research going?" he asked me.

"Okay." I sighed. "But for work that's supposed to be so arty, there's an awful lot of business involved."

"Do you think you're gonna move to L.A.?" Mallory asked abruptly.

I could see that Daddy was going to listen closely to my answer, too.

"Oh, I don't think so," I said. "I think I'll just get as much work in Stamford as I can."

"What happens if you become really famous?" asked Mallory.

"Well," I said, "you never know. I mean, there's a chance I could land a TV series — "

"Any word from the *Swan Lake* folks yet?" Daddy cut in.

"Da-a-ad-dy," I whined. "You *know* that's not till Wednesday."

"Tough wait?" he asked.

"I *hate* waiting!" I practically spit that out. I was surprised at how vehement I sounded.

"I hear you." Daddy smiled. He picked up his briefcase and gave Mallory a reassuring smile.

Then I got on the phone to dial another agent's number. Mallory followed Daddy into the kitchen.

"Do you think she's really going to get on a TV series?" I heard Mallory ask. "I mean, Jessi's my best friend. I'll just *die* if she moves away."

"I think what she really *wants*," Daddy said carefully, "is to dance in *Swan Lake*."

"I do not," I called after them as I dialed the last digits. "I mean, I don't care one way or the other. Anyway, I'm probably not going to get in. So it doesn't matter."

Mallory wandered back into the room and settled back into her place on the couch. I started in on another phone call. Mallory watched me anxiously as I pulled out another index card and started to scribble notes.

CHAPTER 15

Well, *finally*, Wednesday arrived. I hurried home from school, called the theater, asked the question I was dying to ask, and sucked in my breath as I waited for the answer.

The woman on the other end of the phone took about an hour to find the list of people who had made it into the audition and another hour to search for my name on the list. Okay, it might not have been an hour each. Maybe it was more like five minutes. But those five minutes were *long*. To me, each one could've been a century.

"Ramsey, Ramsey," the woman muttered, as she looked down the list. "What did you say your first name was?"

"Jessi," I said. "Well, I'm probably listed as Jessica."

"Yes, here you are," said the woman. "Jessica Ramsey."

"But what does that mean?" I asked anxiously. "Is my name on the list of cuts or did I get into the show?"

"You're in," she said simply. "Congratulations."

"All *right!*" I yelled. I knew that that was not the most delicate thing to do, but I couldn't help it. "Thank you very much," I babbled. "Thank you very, very much."

I hung up the phone and stood there beaming.

Mama had heard my screech and came into the room.

"You made it?" she asked.

I couldn't even answer. I just nodded.

"Oh, honey, congratulations!" Mama gave me a warm hug.

"So what part did you get?" she asked me. "Are you one of the swan maidens?"

"Oh, my gosh!" I laughed. "I forgot to ask. I guess I'll have to call the theater back. Now that woman'll *really* think I'm nuts."

Mama stayed by my side while I dialed again and asked the question.

"I wondered if you were going to call back." The woman chuckled. "Yes, you're in the corps. You're one of the swan maidens."

"Ask for the rehearsal schedule," Mama prompted.

"Oh, right." At that moment I would've had

trouble remembering my own name. "And when do rehearsals start?"

The woman gave me all the necessary information. I repeated it and Mama wrote it down.

Of course, as soon as I hung up, I called Mallory right away.

"I'm a swan!" I cried into the phone.

"I knew it all along," she said. I could practically hear her grinning into the receiver.

Shortly after I got off the phone with Mallory, Daddy came home from work, early again.

"I hear we've got a ballerina in the house," he said, smiling.

I ran to his arms and he caught me up.

"I'm so happy, Daddy," I said. "I wanted this so badly."

"You think I didn't know that?" He smiled. "All that modeling and agent business didn't fool me for a moment. You were going so far in the other direction, I knew *Swan Lake* must've meant a lot. So much that you couldn't even admit it to yourself."

"Oh, yeah. The modeling stuff," I mused. As soon as I'd heard that I'd gotten into the show, I'd forgotten about those calls to the agents in Stamford. That whole world had just fled my mind.

Daddy went on. "I think sometimes if we want something too badly, we have to play tricks on ourselves so that we won't think it matters so much," he said.

"Is that what I was doing?" I asked. How did parents know these things?

"Well, that's what it looked like to me," Daddy said.

Hmm. All those index cards. Suddenly, I didn't have any use for them at all. I was right back where I started from — ballet. And suddenly I knew it was exactly where I belonged, sort of like my true home. I did a couple of quick little jumps and ran down to work at my barre until the club meeting.

It wasn't until later that week that I got to tell Derek that I had made *Swan Lake* after all. I decided not to call him up, that it would be better if I went over and told him in person. That way I'd also get to say my good-byes.

One afternoon after school, I stopped by the Masterses' house. It was kind of sad to go there and see that they were really moving out again. Of course, since they were going to keep the house, they were leaving all their furniture and everything, but there were lots of boxes and suitcases scattered around, and Mrs. Masters had put sheets over the chairs in the living room. The place looked kind of ghostlike.

"Derek will be so glad to see you," Mrs. Masters said as she let me in. "Derek!" she called upstairs. "You've got a visitor!"

Derek came bounding down the steps.

"Jessi!" he cried. "I was hoping you'd come over."

Derek grabbed me by the hand and dragged me up to his room, which looked every bit as strange as the living room had. Derek's clothes were all over the bed, and beside them was an open suitcase.

"I'm packing," he said.

"I can see. When are you leaving?"

"Tomorrow morning," said Derek.

"Gee, it seems like you just got here."

"Well, maybe you'll be coming out to L.A. soon yourself," Derek said hopefully.

"I wouldn't count on that," I said. I tried to sound as gentle as I could.

"Who knows, though?" Derek went on. "The agents in Stamford sent *me* to L.A."

How was I going to tell him?

"I don't think I'll be working with those agents," I started to explain.

"What?" Derek said. "But you told me you'd made a million phone calls."

"That's true. I did," I said with a sigh. "But

then something happened. I made *Swan Lake*."

"You did!" Derek cried. "Great, Jessi! I knew you'd make it! Ever since I heard those other ballerinas tearing you apart."

"It is great." I smiled. "But once I got in, I realized that ballet is the thing I really love. I want to be a ballerina, not a model or an actress. I've already put so much time and work into dance."

Derek's face fell.

"So now you won't ever come to L.A.," he said. He looked so forlorn, that I laughed all of a sudden.

"Never say never," I said. "And besides, you'll be coming back to Stoneybrook sometimes. And now when you come you've got friends, and you know the kids in school. . . ."

"Yeah," Derek agreed. "Thanks to the Baby-sitters Club." He was starting to cheer up. "Thanks again for the party, Jessi. It was great. No one ever threw me a surprise party before."

I thought back to that morning and how nice it had been to watch Derek with his friends. That reminded me.

"Oh, yeah, Derek," I said. "Listen, I've been meaning to ask you. I thought you said that John Superbrat was in your class. But there was no John on your class list. What ever happened with that kid? Did he stop bullying you?"

"John?" Derek said quickly. His eyes shifted away from mine.

"Yeah. John. Is he in another grade?"

"No, he's the same grade," Derek said slowly.

"A different class then?"

Derek gulped and started fiddling with a string hanging from his bedspread.

"No, he's even in the same class," he answered.

"Well, why wasn't he on the list?" I persisted. "You mean, we gave all the kids invitations except him?"

"Sort of," Derek said vaguely. "But he was at the party anyway."

"He was at the party?" I cried. "John? The Superbrat? He was *there?*"

"Jessi, let's go downstairs," Derek said quickly. "Maybe Todd wants to say goodbye."

"Wait a minute, Derek," I said. "Why are you trying to change the subject? Did something awful happen with John? You have to tell me now."

Derek sat there a long time before he opened his mouth again.

"It was kind of awful," he said. "John's an awful kind of kid."

"What did he do?" I pressed. "And how could he have been at the party?"

"Jessi," Derek said. He lowered his voice to almost a whisper. "I hate to tell you this. It's really embarrassing. *I* was John. And all those things I said John did? Well, I did them."

"What?" What in the world was Derek talking about? I didn't get it at all.

Derek went on.

"See, what happened," he said, "was that the kids were bothering me so much that I had to get back at them. So whenever they did something mean to me, I started doing mean things back to them."

"Well, why'd you say it was John?" I asked.

"I don't know." Derek shook his head. "When I told you, it was like I had to tell somebody what I'd been doing, but I didn't really know how to tell. And then once the boys started actually being friends with me, I didn't have to do those things anymore. So John just kind of disappeared."

"*You* tied a kid's shoes together in gym?" I was still incredulous. "*You* dumped someone's books all over the playground?"

Derek nodded sheepishly. "Only because I

wanted to make friends so badly," he said.

Suddenly I started to giggle. The idea of trying to make friends by dumping over someone's book bag was just too silly. Before I knew it, I was laughing pretty hard. It was contagious. Derek started laughing, too.

"Hey," I teased, "I'll be your best friend if you tie my shoes together."

Derek doubled over. After awhile, when we both quieted down, Derek's face grew thoughtful.

"It was horrible," he admitted. "I didn't *want* to do those things. I guess you make more friends by being nice to people, don't you?"

"That's usually how it's done," I said, and smiled.

"Well, now I know," said Derek. "I guess I'll only be that mean again if somebody writes it into a script for me."

"Good idea," I said, laughing.

It looked like it was time to go. I was dreading our good-byes.

"So, Derek," I said. "Good luck out there. Break a leg and everything. Send me a postcard if you get a chance."

"Oh, I almost forgot!" Derek jumped up. He opened his dresser drawer and pulled out a large envelope. He handed it to me.

"Open it up," he said proudly.

Inside the envelope was one of Derek's head shots. His smiling face was staring right out at me. In the bottom corner, he had inscribed the photo:

"TO JESSI, YOU'RE THE BEST BABY-SITTER I EVER HAD. AND YOU'RE A PRETTY GOOD BALLERINA, TOO. GOOD LUCK WITH YOUR TOUR JETAYS. YOUR FRIEND FOREVER, DEREK MASTERS."

I gave Derek a big hug good-bye and hurried out of the house. I aleady felt kind of choked up and I didn't want to start crying.

When I got halfway down the street I stopped and pulled the photo out to look at it again.

"Your friend forever," it said.

Well, who could tell? Maybe that would end up being true. Anyway, it had sure been fun being friends with Derek so far. I slipped the photo back into its envelope and started to run home. After all, I had a lot of index cards to throw out. . . .

And, hey, I thought as I leaped over the curb, I had *Swan Lake* to learn, too!

About the Author

ANN M. MARTIN did *a lot* of baby-sitting when she was growing up in Princeton, New Jersey. Now her favorite baby-sitting charge is her cat, Mouse, who lives with her in her Manhattan apartment.

Ann Martin's Apple Paperbacks are *Bummer Summer, Inside Out, Stage Fright, Me and Katie (the Pest)*, and all the other books in the Baby-sitters Club series.

She is a former editor of books for children, and was graduated from Smith College. She likes ice cream, the beach, and *I Love Lucy*; and she hates to cook.

THE BABY-SITTERS CLUB

Look for #28

WELCOME BACK, STACEY!

The elevator doors opened. I stepped into the hallway and paused, listening. The only sound was the TV blaring in 12C.

I walked to my apartment on tiptoe, stopping every few feet.

At 12E I listened especially carefully. Nothing.

I found my key, slipped it in the lock, and let myself inside. A tiny part of me was afraid that something had happened, that Mom or Dad had stormed off. But, no. They were sitting in the living room. They didn't look like they were doing much of anything, so they must have been talking.

Whew. If they were talking, that meant they weren't fighting.

"Hi, Mom. Hi, Dad," I said casually, as if I hadn't heard the fight, and hadn't been to Laine's.

"Hi, honey," they replied at the same time.

137

Another good sign. Speaking in unison.

But then Mom said, "Stacey, we need to talk to you."

Whoa, bad sign.

"You do?" I desperately hoped that they were going to accuse me of not sticking to my diet. I even hoped that my English teacher had called up personally to tell my parents about the D I'd gotten on a quiz.

No such luck. I sat down on the edge of a couch and looked at Mom and Dad, who were glancing at each other as if to say, "You go first." "No, *you* go first."

Finally, Mom went first. "I guess it's no secret," she said, "that your dad and I have been having some problems."

No secret? The whole building probably knew.

"Well, I have heard you, um, arguing a lot lately," I admitted.

Mom nodded. "And we've decided to do something about it. Stacey, your father and I are getting a divorce."

"What?" I whispered.

"We're getting a divorce," Dad spoke up.

I felt as if someone had slapped me across the face.

THE BABY-SITTERS CLUB®

by Ann M. Martin

More titles... ➤

The Baby-sitters Club titles continued...

☐ MG43568-X	#39 Poor Mallory!	$3.25
☐ MG44082-9	#40 Claudia and the Middle School Mystery	$3.25
☐ MG43570-1	#41 Mary Anne Versus Logan	$3.25
☐ MG44083-7	#42 Jessi and the Dance School Phantom	$3.25
☐ MG43572-8	#43 Stacey's Emergency	$3.25
☐ MG43573-6	#44 Dawn and the Big Sleepover	$3.25
☐ MG43574-4	#45 Kristy and the Baby Parade	$3.25
☐ MG43569-8	#46 Mary Anne Misses Logan	$3.25
☐ MG44971-0	#47 Mallory on Strike	$3.25
☐ MG43571-X	#48 Jessi's Wish	$3.25
☐ MG44970-2	#49 Claudia and the Genius of Elm Street	$3.25
☐ MG44969-9	#50 Dawn's Big Date	$3.25
☐ MG44968-0	#51 Stacey's Ex-Best Friend	$3.25
☐ MG44966-4	#52 Mary Anne + 2 Many Babies	$3.25
☐ MG44967-2	#53 Kristy for President	$3.25
☐ MG44965-6	#54 Mallory and the Dream Horse	$3.25
☐ MG44964-8	#55 Jessi's Gold Medal	$3.25
☐ MG45575-3	Logan's Story Special Edition Readers' Request	$3.25
☐ MG44240-6	Baby-sitters on Board! Super Special #1	$3.50
☐ MG44239-2	Baby-sitters' Summer Vacation Super Special #2	$3.50
☐ MG43973-1	Baby-sitters' Winter Vacation Super Special #3	$3.50
☐ MG42493-9	Baby-sitters' Island Adventure Super Special #4	$3.50
☐ MG43575-2	California Girls! Super Special #5	$3.50
☐ MG43576-0	New York, New York! Super Special #6	$3.50
☐ MG44963-X	Snowbound Super Special #7	$3.50
☐ MG44962-X	Baby-sitters at Shadow Lake Super Special #8	$3.50

Available wherever you buy books...or use this order form.

Scholastic Inc., P.O. Box 7502, 2931 E. McCarty Street, Jefferson City, MO 65102

Please send me the books I have checked above. I am enclosing $_____
(please add $2.00 to cover shipping and handling). Send check or money order - no
cash or C.O.D.s please.

Name _____

Address _____

City_____ State/Zip _____

Please allow four to six weeks for delivery. Offer good in the U.S. only. Sorry, mail orders are not
available to residents of Canada. Prices subject to change.

BSC1291